Killing Eve

TV Milestones

Series Editor

Barry Keith Grant, Brock University

TV Milestones is part of the Contemporary Approaches to Film and Media Series.

A complete listing of the books in this series can be found online at wsupress.wayne.edu.

Killing Eve

Clare Sears

Wayne State University Press
Detroit

ISBN 9780814351697 (paperback)
ISBN 9780814351703 (ebook)

Library of Congress Control Number: 2026935518

Cover image © Pelagjia / Shutterstock.com.

Published with the assistance of a fund established by Thelma Gray James of Wayne State University.

Wayne State University Press rests on Waawiyaataanong, also referred to as Detroit, the ancestral and contemporary homeland of the Three Fires Confederacy. These sovereign lands were granted by the Ojibwe, Odawa, Potawatomi, and Wyandot Nations, in 1807, through the Treaty of Detroit. Wayne State University Press affirms Indigenous sovereignty and honors all tribes with a connection to Detroit. With our Native neighbors, the press works to advance educational equity and promote a better future for the earth and all people.

Wayne State University Press
Leonard N. Simons Building
4809 Woodward Avenue
Detroit, Michigan 48201-1309

Visit us online at wsupress.wayne.edu.

CONTENTS

ACKNOWLEDGMENTS

First, I am deeply grateful to Sally Woodward Gentle and Phoebe Waller-Bridge for participating in this project. Their generosity, time, and trust greatly enhanced my analysis of *Killing Eve* and made the writing process much more fun. I also thank Debbie Idowu and Emma Holman for their help in facilitating the interviews.

Second, I am eternally grateful to my friends in the *Killing Eve* fandom, whose ideas, creativity, and commitments to queer media sparked my interest in writing this book. I owe special thanks to Anya, Landrie, Katya, Kate, Laura, Henry, Chasey, Dina, Sari Katharyn, Jamie, and Del for sharing their skills and knowledge with me.

Third, I am indebted to the many academic friends and colleagues who helped shape this book. I particularly thank Andreana Clay and Celine Parreñas Shimizu for reading and responding to earlier versions of the manuscript, and Barbara Barnes, Maya Deane, Ikaika Gleisberg and Jen Reck for countless conversations about the cultural meanings of *Killing Eve*. I'm also grateful to my students and colleagues at San Francisco State University for their consistent energy and inspiration, particularly Sarah Bakker, Chris Bettinger, Angela Fillingim, Valerie Francisco-Menchavez, Hülya Gürtuna, Erik Hidalgo, Alexis Martinez, Rita Meléndez, and Ryan Moore. I'm also thankful for the sabbatical funding that gave me time to write this book.

This project would not have materialized without the editorial prowess of Marie Sweetman. At the 2022 American Studies Association conference, Marie encouraged me to write this book, and she has been an unwavering source of support ever since. I'm also immensely grateful to the anonymous peer reviewers whose generous insights enriched my work, and to Sandra Korn, Carrie Teefey, Katie Martelle, Emily Gauronskas, and Emily Shelton for their guidance during the publication process.

Killing Eve is a television show about obsession, and I became duly obsessed. I am deeply grateful to my family for indulging my endless talk about the series, particularly my children, Joaquin and Francisco, as well as my parents, Brenda and Colin, who shared in my excitement when I visited Sid Gentle Films in London and kept me updated on *Killing Eve* mentions in the UK press. Finally, I thank my partner, Tia, for her endless brilliance, kindness, curiosity, and love. Life is long (if we're lucky), and I'm thrilled to go through it with her.

INTRODUCTION

In the opening scene of *Killing Eve*, Villanelle—a young and stylish Russian assassin—exits a café in Vienna and petulantly tips a bowl of ice cream into the lap of a small child. Moments later, Eve Polastri—a middle-aged Korean American MI5 agent—wakes up screaming in bed in London, after falling asleep on her arms. When *Killing Eve* premiered in 2018, these two scenes instantly signaled that this was no ordinary spy thriller show. Wickedly funny and seriously smart, *Killing Eve* upended thriller conventions with its style, wit, and laser-sharp focus on magnetic women. It also redeployed genre tropes to produce a new form of queer television. Centering the obsessive, erotic, and deeply compelling relationship between Eve and Villanelle, *Killing Eve* transformed the television landscape by appropriating thriller conventions to explore the complexity and queerness of women's desires.

Killing Eve burst onto television screens in April 2018 and ended after four seasons in April 2022. Created by Phoebe Waller-Bridge for Sid Gentle Films, the show was a runaway success, smashing viewership records, captivating critics, and winning multiple industry awards. Anchored in the cat-and-mouse chase central to many crime and spy thrillers, *Killing Eve* dazzled viewers with its lush aesthetics and groundbreaking portrayal of queer sexualities. The show enjoyed immense popularity among LGBTQ+ audiences, quickly establishing itself as must-see TV. It also attracted significant controversy that centered on queerbaiting strategies, the "bury your gays" trope, and the persistent centering of whiteness on-screen.

This book is the first to explore *Killing Eve*'s place in television history. It draws on my exclusive interviews with Phoebe Waller-Bridge (creator and writer) and Sally Woodward Gentle (executive producer), as well as in-depth analysis of key scenes. Focusing on the show's innovations—and the controversies it sometimes sparked—I argue that *Killing Eve* matters in television history due to its appropriation of thriller conventions to center women's queer desires.

Killing Eve's queer subversions of the cat-and-mouse thriller transformed the television landscape. It wasn't, however, the first show to rework the thriller for alternate ends. As I elaborate in chapter 1, the genre heavily skews toward men who pursue each other as spy against spy, assassin against agent, or serial killer against cop. In recent years, several shows have disrupted the genre's default masculinity by featuring women investigators in pursuit of dangerous men: Stella Gibson in *The Fall* (RTÉ One/BBC Two, 2013–16), for instance, or Catherine Cawood in *Happy Valley* (BBC One, 2014–23). Far fewer shows have featured women as the villains to be pursued. Certainly, spy thrillers sometimes include women assassins, but these are typically femme fatales with tragic backstories rather than fully developed antagonists. Television shows rarely cast women as psychopathic killers, with *Luther*'s Alice Morgan a notable exception (BBC One, 2010–19), and none had featured a cat-and-mouse chase between two women, until *Killing Eve*.

Killing Eve centers the complex relationship between Eve Polastri (Sandra Oh), a forty-something Korean American woman working for UK security services, and Villanelle Astankova (Jodie Comer), a young, flamboyant, white Russian assassin who works for a global crime syndicate called the Twelve, under the watch of her handler, Konstantin Vasiliev (Kim Bodnia). When Carolyn Martens (Fiona Shaw) of MI6 hires Eve to track Villanelle in an unofficial investigation, the two

Killing Eve's subversion of the cat-and-mouse thriller brings Eve and Villanelle into close proximity, as season 2's kitchen scene illustrates ("Smell Ya Later," 2.5).

women soon develop an all-consuming mutual obsession, pursuing each other with longing, envy, and spiraling desire. As *Killing Eve* reworked the cat-and-mouse narrative into an offbeat queer love story, its central question was not "Will she catch her?" but "What will happen when she does?" Throughout the series, sex and murder were equally plausible, with either woman coming out on top.

By routing the cat-and-mouse thriller's signature chase through women characters, *Killing Eve* brought to the surface the sublimated sexual tension that often animates the genre. Moreover, it actively hijacked genre tropes to stage its exploration of queer desires. Despite its potentially sobering subject matter, *Killing Eve* was chaotic and playful, undercutting a serious plot with biting humor that poked fun at thriller conventions. It also delivered psychological depth in surprising and moving ways. In doing so, it opened up new pleasures within a genre that often restricts women to victim roles.

The opening scenes of the pilot episode ("Nice Face," 1.1) enact these interests. While crime thrillers frequently launch with a scene of a screaming woman, *Killing Eve*'s opening horror is far more mundane: Eve has fallen asleep on her arms. The scene orients viewers to *Killing Eve*'s humor and clever subversion of thriller tropes. It also introduces us to Eve in the midst of her regular life, in bed with her husband, after a night of karaoke with friends. With hindsight, however, Eve's first scene also hints at what is to come, capturing the tingling thrill and disorientation of waking up, blood rushing to parts of the body that sleep has rendered numb.

Killing Eve centrally explores the excitement and terror of waking up from mundane middle-aged existence to claim *more*, however defined, whatever the cost. The show's creators positioned Eve as viewers' entryway into this journey. At the start of the series, we find her stable but chafing against the monotony of everyday life. Her desk job bores her. Her husband bores her. She longs for excitement, even trouble, but, as she grumbles in the pilot, "trouble's not interested in me." In early publicity interviews, Waller-Bridge and Woodward Gentle described Eve as an "everywoman." However, this characterization is spliced with strangeness from the start. As a self-described fan of female assassins who fantasizes about dismembering her husband and stuffing his body into the blender, Eve is a whirlwind character: brilliant, stubborn, willful, impulsive, and willing to throw her life away when Villanelle crosses her path. Building on the popularity of true crime television, *Killing Eve* aligns viewers with Eve's perspective, inviting us to take voyeuristic pleasure in Villanelle's antics and asking how far we will go in indulging the magnetic killer.

It is a tantalizing question. Villanelle is a young, queer, and audacious assassin: stylish, childish, charming, terrifying, and outrageously fun to watch. With a love of fashion and flair for dramatics, Villanelle's kills are often stylized and highly inventive. She also can be playful and cruel, delighting in pranks at others' expense. Her opening scene is particularly instructive, as she eats ice cream in a Vienna café, fashionably dressed and surrounded by upscale shopping bags. The scene is quiet, without dialogue, but layered with hints that something is wrong: Villanelle struggles to exchange smiles with a young girl at another table; she resorts to mimicry to perform what should be a natural act; she wipes a drop of blood from her wristwatch; and, finally, as she leaves the cafe, she tips ice cream into the child's lap. The sequence breaks from genre conventions that typically introduce psychopathic killers via their gruesome murder scenes. *Dexter* (Showtime, 2006–13), for instance, first presents Dexter Morgan abducting, torturing, and murdering a man, bound to a table with plastic wrap, while *Barry* (HBO, 2018–23) introduces Barry Beckham standing near a bullet-rent corpse. In stark contrast, *Killing Eve* chooses ice cream, with evidence of Villanelle's professional violence barely present—just a delicate splash of blood on her wristwatch that she easily wipes away ("Nice Face," 1.1).

On the surface, Villanelle is a fantasy character—Eve's fantasy, to be precise—embodying freedom from societal conventions and moral constraints. But she also is strangely relatable, palpably lonely and yearning for normalcy and closeness that remain out of reach. Although the creators of *Killing Eve* positioned Eve as the primary locus of audience identification—an "everywoman" who rages against heteronormative stagnation—many queer viewers found a greater affinity with Villanelle. The character became a surprising queer icon in popular culture, as fans identified with her style and sexual agency and viewed her psychopathic struggle for connection as emblematic of queer isolation. This audience-driven identification created an alternate entry point into the series, expanding its cultural and emotional reach. It also invited competing perspectives on the series' central "point," as I discuss in chapter 4.

Killing Eve defied easy classification, combining the terror of a fast-paced thriller with twisted comedy and character-driven psychological drama. At its roots, however, it was escapist TV, steeped in play and taboo queer thrills. The show courted a cool, retro spy aesthetic, evoking the style of 1960s television shows like *The Avengers* (ITV, 1961–69) and *I-Spy* (NBC, 1965–68). It also boasted an award-winning soundtrack, grounded in the cinematic sounds of Los Angeles band Unloved, combined with an eclectic mix of obscure, international tracks: pop songs that made light of danger, torch songs on the glamour of murder, and rock 'n' roll tracks about the devil's charms. Despite its frequent displays of violence, *Killing Eve* was tonally light, with a complete disregard for moral concerns. The show took place in a slightly off-kilter cultural universe that sometimes cited morality and legality but did not let them impede the fun. The result was an exhilarating and somewhat anarchic viewing experience, slightly detached from reality and time.

Killing Eve's genre transgressions produced not only a new type of thriller, but also a new type of queer TV. Premiering in 2018, it joined an impressive wave of groundbreaking shows that brought more queer and trans women of color to the screen than ever before. Most notably, *Pose* (FX, 2018–21) rose to prominence as an award-winning drama about New York's Black and Latine ballroom scene during the 1980s, making television history with its large-scale casting of transgender actors in recurring roles. *Vida* (Starz, 2018–20) also carved new paths as a sex-positive comedy-drama centered on two Mexican American sisters navigating gentrification, queerness, and belonging in East LA. From the political history of *A Very English Scandal* (BBC One/Amazon Prime Video, 2018) to the first Black lesbian superhero in *Black Lightning* (The CW, 2018–21), the year marked a notable expansion in television's attention to LGBTQ+ history, community, family, and identity.

Killing Eve's queer innovations took place on a different register, hijacking a traditionally masculine and heterosexual genre to center women's same-gender desires. Unlike most queer television, *Killing Eve* bracketed questions of identity to dive deep into attraction, unconstrained by its significations. It also centered kink dynamics and developed innovative techniques to bring "unsayable" desires into view. Without the container of identity, same-gender desire in *Killing Eve* did not serve a coming-out narrative or function as positive representation. Instead, it simmered in messy complexity, saturated with dread, excitement, horror, compulsion, confusion, and tenderness—often all at the same time.

Killing Eve's distinctive approach to sexuality was not without controversy, and the show sometimes found itself embroiled in debates about queer representation on-screen. While these debates often stemmed from fan disappointment with specific storytelling choices, they also reflected television's role as a site for cultural debate. Consequently, instead of viewing these controversies as stains on *Killing Eve*'s reputation, I consider them to be evidence of its cultural importance as milestone TV.

Methods

This book draws from multiple sources. First, I analyze scenes from the show. I draw most often from season 1, which established the series' tonal template, but I also include later seasons as they relate to the book's central claims. Second, I include information from interviews that I conducted with Sally Woodward Gentle and Phoebe Waller-Bridge in 2024 and 2025.[1] Both women offered new insights into the show's making and meanings and spoke on the record about *Killing Eve* for the first time since its end. Lastly, I incorporate popular media coverage of the show, including published interviews with creators and cast. As I discuss in chapter 4, published interviews take place under numerous constraints, primarily serving as marketing tools. I include them here as supplementary texts that extended *Killing Eve*'s cultural meanings, not as direct reflections of creative intent.

Throughout the book, my analysis draws on several concepts from television studies and cultural studies. First, I approach television shows as polysemic, which means they have multiple meanings that may exceed creators' intentions. Specifically, I build on insights from sociologist Stuart Hall to distinguish between the "preferred meanings" that TV creators encode in their shows, and the received or "negotiated meanings" that viewers take away.[2] Since these meanings need not align, audiences and creators can understand the same show in different ways. In the book, I explore both sets of meanings, as well as occasional tensions between the two. My goal is not to judge who was "right," but to explore the ways that meaning is always in motion—produced, contested, and circulated—via the medium of television.

Second, I distinguish between "quality TV" and "milestone TV." The former describes a historically specific form of programming that emerged in the 2000s, when HBO began marketing dramas such as *The Sopranos* (HBO, 1999–2007) and *The Wire* (HBO, 2002–8) as "prestige" television. These shows were characterized by big budgets, complex storylines, and cinematic production; they also were oriented toward men. TV scholar Júlia Havas has tracked the subsequent rise of "feminist quality TV" in the 2010s, and *Killing Eve* could be analyzed in relation to that trend.[3] In this book, however, I pivot away from quality TV to instead focus on milestone TV. Milestone TV is television that significantly impacts the media landscape or popular culture, by opening doors for future programming, reshaping audience expectations, or inciting meaningful cultural debates. Consequently, I only consider questions of "quality" as they intersect with *Killing Eve*'s cultural significance.

Finally, I draw on the framework of disidentification to analyze *Killing Eve* as innovative, imperfect television. As formulated by performance studies scholar José Esteban Muñoz, disidentification refers to the ways that racially and sexually marginalized groups can navigate dominant media texts by strategically reworking harmful and exclusionary messages, often through subcultural artistic performances.[4] Rooted in queer of color practice, disidentification also works as an analytic method that sets aside simple acceptance or full rejection of media texts, to highlight what can be extracted, critiqued, and reworked. Although queer of color artistic reworkings of *Killing Eve* are beyond the scope of this book, I use the concept of disidentification to interrogate the series' innovations and imperfections when representing sexuality and race.[5] I do so as a white queer academic, mindful of the limits and insights that my positionality entails. Specifically, my analysis takes *Killing Eve*'s shortfalls seriously without dismissing its contributions and affirms the show's lasting value without minimizing its limitations.

Anchored in these sources and concepts, my book examines *Killing Eve*'s place within television history. It analyzes textual meanings, viewer responses, and the broader industry and cultural contexts in which the series was produced and viewed. The book is enriched by my interviews with *Killing Eve*'s creators, who spoke at length about the show's style and tone (chapter 1), queerness and kink (chapter 2), depictions of psychopaths (chapter 3), and controversial ending (chapter 4). Woodward Gentle and Waller-Bridge also provided behind-the-scenes insights into *Killing Eve*'s early development, which I turn to now.

Development

Killing Eve was a major international success, commissioned and aired by BBC America, and distributed by Endeavor Content in over 140 countries. Despite its eventual acclaim, however, the show faced significant challenges during its early development. These obstacles underscore both the show's groundbreaking nature and the crucial role of industry conditions in determining which programs are made.

Killing Eve originated in a series of novellas by Luke Jennings, an established UK author, whose previous fiction had been nominated for the prestigious Man Booker Prize. The first novella, *Codename Villanelle*, was published with Amazon in February 2014, followed by *Villanelle: Hollowpoint* (2014), *Villanelle: Shanghai* (2015), and *Odessa* (2016). At Amazon's invitation, Jennings had created the series for Kindle Singles, the company's new self-publishing venture. Shortly after the first novella's release, Sally Woodward Gentle, of Sid Gentle Films, obtained a copy from a colleague. Intrigued by Jennings's rerouting of a traditional spy story through two women characters, Woodward Gentle optioned the series to adapt for television.[6]

As a book-to-screen adaptation, *Killing Eve* aligned with recent trends in the television industry. Although such adaptations are not new, their presence has surged since 2013, when Netflix began using published books as a primary source for its original programming. Book-to-screen adaptations have also evolved qualitatively, as producers look beyond bestsellers and earlier standards of textual fidelity for compelling stories to transform for television.[7] The book-to-screen adaptation model also fit within the wheelhouse of Sid Gentle Films, a small independent production company founded by Woodward Gentle, Lee Morris, and Henrietta Colvin in 2013. Before *Killing Eve*, Sid Gentle Films had produced several book-based dramas, including *The Durrells* (ITV, 2016–19), *SS-GB* (BBC One, 2017), and *Likely Stories* (Sky Arts, 2016). As Woodward Gentle explained in an interview with *The Hollywood Reporter*: "That's what my job is—to find IP, put clever people with it and then see what happens."[8]

For *Killing Eve*, that clever person would be Phoebe Waller-Bridge. In 2014, Waller-Bridge was dazzling UK theater audiences with her stage play, *Fleabag*, which had debuted at the Edinburgh Fringe in 2013 before launching a run at London's Soho Theater the following year. Woodward Gentle met Waller-Bridge after reading her play, and they bonded over a shared love of Fuerza Bruta, an Argentine postmodern stunt-dance troupe performing at London's Roundhouse Theater. Waller-Bridge was not yet an established television writer—her debut shows, *Fleabag* (BBC Three/Amazon Prime Video, 2016–19) and *Crashing* (Channel 4, 2016) would not screen until 2016—but Woodward Gentle was drawn to her wicked humor, off-kilter brand of sexual politics, and creative excitement about television as a medium. Anticipating Waller-Bridge's prowess as a genre-defying television writer, Woodward Gentle brought her on to adapt the *Villanelle* novellas.

Working with Sid Gentle Films, Waller-Bridge initially wrote a pilot

script for Sky Living, a UK channel that had expressed early interest in the series. As Woodward Gentle explained to me, Sky Living encouraged the team to create a show so distinctive that "no other channel would want it," only to reject the project in April 2015. Woodward Gentle then pitched the show to multiple networks, including the BBC and Channel 4, but executives struggled to grasp the concept, particularly the character of Villanelle. To make the project more legible, the team sharpened its focus on Eve and changed the title from *Villanelle* to *Killing Eve*. Networks, however, remained skeptical of the show's unconventional approach to genre and gender. As Phoebe Waller-Bridge explained to me:

> When we were trying to sell the show, we had many rejections on the basis that they didn't understand Villanelle as a character and found it hard to care about her. I think that's what compelled and delighted me about her. A young woman doing exactly what she wants, without apology, without shame . . . it inspired me . . . she inspired Eve. I think it played on the idea of how discombobulating a totally self-serving female character is.

Villanelle, of course, would become a fan-favorite character, establishing the viability of such roles and paving the way for future shows. Back in 2015, however, her illegibility posed a major obstacle. As Woodward Gentle described, *Killing Eve* was almost "the one that got away," until a pivotal meeting with BBC America led to a mutually beneficial deal. The partnership reflected not only Woodward Gentle's persistence and vision, but also larger industry shifts and new definitions of commercial success.

While Sid Gentle Films struggled to sell *Killing Eve*, BBC America faced challenges of its own, as it strove to adapt to rapidly changing industry conditions. Jointly owned by BBC Studios and AMC Networks, BBC America was a US basic cable network that traditionally featured UK programming in the United States. The advent of streaming sites, however, had threatened the network's market niche, providing US viewers with multiple new ways to access UK shows. In response, BBC America pursued a new strategy of commissioning original scripted programs, with particular interest in cutting-edge shows with boutique appeal. In the 2010s, such shows became commercially viable, as streaming, cable, and pay-per-view TV dramatically increased the number of available programs while decreasing the expected audience for any one show. In this context, industry definitions of commercial success shifted, making space for niche shows that could cultivate small but loyal fan bases. In 2015, BBC America was specifically searching for an off-beat, feminist, hybrid show to replicate the success of *Orphan Black* (Space/BBC America, 2013–17), a Canadian/UK mash-up that became a cult hit through its women-centered reimagining of the traditional sci-fi genre.

When Woodward Gentle met with BBC America's Melissa Wells in 2016, it became clear that *Killing Eve* fit these parameters. Wells brought the script to BBC America's executive team: Sarah Barnett, Nena Rodrigue, and Gina Mingacci (who later became a producer of *Killing Eve*). The all-women leadership team was rare in the industry and willing to gamble on innovative feminist programs, having already overseen *Orphan Black* and *Top of the Lake* (BBC Two/Sundance TV, 2013–17). In November 2016, BBC America greenlit *Killing Eve* and fast-tracked production, responding to *Fleabag*'s television success and Phoebe Waller-Bridge's emergence as one of the medium's hottest writers. As president Sarah Barnett explained to *The Los Angeles Times*, *Killing Eve* was risky to commission, but, "as TV viewing increasingly fragments, and there are 500-plus scripted shows, you have to take those kinds of risks."[9]

When *Killing Eve* premiered in the US on April 8, 2018, it quickly became clear that the risk had paid off. The show emerged as the breakout hit of the spring, achieving a record-breaking 86 percent increase in viewership from its first to final episode. Five months later, upon its UK premiere on BBC Three, it became BBC iPlayer's most requested series ever, with over 49 million requests. *Killing Eve* went on to dominate the 2019 industry awards, sweeping the BAFTAs and collecting Golden Globe, Peabody, Screen Actors Guild, Writers Guild, and Critics Choice awards.[10] Sandra Oh's recognition was particularly groundbreaking, as she became the first lead actress of Asian descent to be nominated for an Emmy; the first woman of Asian descent to win multiple Golden Globes (following a previous award for *Grey's Anatomy*); and the first woman of Asian descent to win a Golden Globe for Best Actress in a TV Drama in thirty-nine years. The show also dazzled television critics, appearing on more "best of the year" lists than any other series, as well as "best of the decade" and "best of the century" lists compiled by *The New York Times* and *The Guardian*.[11]

Killing Eve's immense success was clearly informed by the talent and labor behind its creation. It also reflected a tight alignment with the broader political and cultural mood. In 2018, both the UK and the US were facing a tide of rising nationalism and right-wing governments, two years into Brexit negotiations and Trump's first presidential term. Both countries were also witnessing the rise of the #MeToo and Time's Up movements, as women protested the ubiquity of sexual violence and harassment, particularly by powerful men. *Killing Eve* spoke to the anger of this moment. Its central characters were brilliant, awful, raucous women, who tore through life without apology or explanation. Led by women on- and off-screen, the show refused to entertain sexual violence or feature plotlines where women used sex as a means to an end. Despite its focus on murder and mayhem, *Killing Eve* was strangely inspiring, staging a defiant challenge to the forces that constrain women's desires, meeting the energy of the time.

Subsequent seasons strove to match season 1's glory, with varied success. Season 2 arguably came closest, with positive reviews and multiple award nominations, but reactions to seasons 3 and 4 were mixed, as critics and fans claimed that the show had lost its spark, even as viewership remained high. Recognizing that *Killing Eve* rested on a time-limited premise, Woodward Gentle began thinking of how to wrap up the show at season 2's end, and she entered informal discussions with BBC America during the making of season 3. It wasn't until March 2021, however, several episodes into the development of season 4, that Sid Gentle Films and BBC America announced that season 4 would be the last.

Synopsis

Although *Killing Eve* had a loose and unwieldy plot concerning political assassinations and intrigue, this primarily functioned as a backdrop for the show's main concern: the relationship between Eve and Villanelle. This relationship stretched across four seasons, each written by a different lead writer: Phoebe Waller-Bridge (season 1), Emerald Fennell (season 2), Suzanne Heathcote (season 3), and Laura Neal (season 4). Although lead writer rotation is relatively common in anthology series (e.g., *American Crime Story*, FX, 2016–present), it's far less typical in longform television that follows a continuous storyline across multiple seasons. Sid Gentle Films adopted this unusual approach when Waller-Bridge left to write the second season of *Fleabag*. As I discuss in chapter 4, this approach had mixed results, occasionally muddling vision and tone. Nonetheless, the themes that concern me in this book remained present throughout the series. I briefly summarize each season below.

In season 1, Eve is recruited by Carolyn Martens to track Villanelle in an off-the-books MI6 operation. The two women quickly develop a mutual obsession, as Villanelle gleefully kills her way across Europe, and Eve matches her daring, step-by-step. The erotically charged cat-and-mouse chase (or "cat-and-cat," as some viewers noted) climaxes in the season finale, when Eve tracks Villanelle to her Paris flat, confesses feelings, and lures Villanelle into bed, only to stab her in the stomach. Eve then instantly changes her mind and scrambles to fix the damage she has caused, but Villanelle escapes.

Villanelle stabs a man in the eye with a poisonous hairpin for her first featured kill, accompanied by a flamboyant song by Pshycotic Beats, "Killer Shangri-Lah" ("Nice Face," 1.1).

The season establishes *Killing Eve*'s tonal template: clever, stylish, wickedly funny, and packed with outrageous kills. In episode 1, Villanelle stabs a mafia boss in the eye with a designer hairpin adorned with two naked women kissing. In episode 2, she uses poisoned perfume to kill an asthmatic fragrance designer, announcing her love of "the breathy ones," and waving bye-bye with the dead woman's hand. Moving beyond the bounds of her job, Villanelle stabs Eve's friend on a Berlin dance floor; runs down her own ex-girlfriend with a car; bites out a prisoner's throat; and embellishes her contracted kill of Eve's boss by castrating and displaying his body in a dress she had gifted to Eve. Hand in hand with over-the-top violence, the season is sly, stylish, and refreshingly playful, laced with a burgeoning queer romance, as the women study each other with voyeuristic interest and growing desire.

Season 2 begins thirty seconds later, as Villanelle staggers, bleeding, through Paris, and Eve heads back to London, stunned by the literal blood on her hands. Both women quickly recover and the show proceeds at pace. Temporarily severing ties with the Twelve, Villanelle freelances as an assassin, while Eve investigates a new case. The women's shared fixation, however, continues to spiral and reaches new heights when Eve takes out a hit on herself to recruit Villanelle for MI6. The pair then head to Rome, where the season ends in spectacular violence, as Eve axes a man to death to save Villanelle's life, only to learn that Villanelle could have saved herself. Against the backdrop of Roman ruins, Villanelle's plans for a romantic getaway end abruptly with more spilt blood: The women argue, Eve leaves, and Villanelle shoots her for dead.

Similar to season 1, season 2 blends humor, drama, and queer erotics, but with its own distinctive tone. The season is more cartoonish, with archetypical male villains replacing season 1's ineffectual men. The comedy is different, too. While season 1 interweaves humor and pathos into key moments, season 2 ricochets between the two, leading viewers down one emotional path, only to pivot at the last minute. The season features *Killing Eve*'s kinkiest scenes, confirming the women's mutual attraction. It also features Villanelle's most theatrical kills. In one episode, she kills a man with a knitting needle and stuffs a toilet brush in his mouth. In another, she dons a pig mask and Swiss dirndl to publicly string up and gut a man, reproducing a gruesome seventeenth-century painting that appears on a postcard she sends to Eve (*The Corpses of the De Witt Brothers*, Jan de Baen, ca. 1672–75). Season 2 amplifies *Killing Eve*'s horror elements, with twisted fairy-tale overtones. As a result, its bloody finale has different effects than season 1's. While Eve's stabbing of Villanelle had moved the plot forward, revealing her new capacity for violence, Villanelle's gunshot closes it down, at least temporarily, confirming Eve's naivety and Villanelle's inability to change.

Season 3 begins six months later, with Eve living alone in New Malden (London's Koreatown) and working in a restaurant kitchen, while Villanelle gets married in Barcelona to a woman she had met after shooting Eve. The death of Carolyn's son, Kenny, however, soon entangles their fates again, even as they spend most of the season apart. Season 3 is radically different from earlier seasons, dialing back the kinky power play and twisted humor to focus on loneliness and loss. It also includes stylistic experiments with nonlinear time, a redeployment of the series' location cards, and even an episode without Eve. The season primarily focuses on Villanelle, as she visits family in Russia, murders her mother, and grows disenchanted with the Twelve. Eve's trajectory is less fleshed out, but nonetheless sees her kill again, intensifying her ties to Villanelle. The season features some of the show's most romantic moments, culminating in a tender scene on Tower Bridge, where the women take responsibility for their own violence and decide to part ways, only to turn back in the closing shot.

Due to COVID-related production delays, viewers waited two years to learn what would happen after the bridge. In a surprising move, however, season 4 drops that storyline and begins with a significant time jump that finds the characters apart again and in their most hostile dynamic yet. Villanelle is particularly broken, attempting to "be good" via organized religion, but experiencing hallucinations (of herself, in drag, as Jesus) that encourage her to kill again. Eve, in turn, is at her most angry, refusing to help Villanelle and solely obsessed with destroying the Twelve. The season recaptures much of the chaos and campiness of earlier seasons. It also is the queerest by far, both in terms of aesthetics and plot. Throughout the season, Eve and Villanelle interact as if they are angry ex-girlfriends, but team up for the final episode, to bring down the Twelve. Here, at last, they come together as an unhinged outlaw duo in love, enjoying a romantic road trip to London before killing the Twelve on the River Thames. Their happiness is short-lived, however, as Villanelle is killed by a sniper in the final minutes, pushing Eve into the river to save her, where Eve resurfaces and screams, alone.

Killing Eve was a wild and provocative television show that transformed the media landscape. In chapter 1, "Chic as Shit," I examine the series' foundational elements, focusing on its distinctive style, characters, and tone.[12] I situate *Killing Eve* in relation to vintage spy shows and cat-and-mouse thrillers, highlighting its innovations and gender subversions. I also critique its approach to race.

In chapter 2, "Define Relationship," I explore the series' groundbreaking approach to queer desire, in contrast with more conventional lesbian television. Specifically, I emphasize same-gender erotics delinked from identity, kink dynamics, and novel techniques for communicating "unsayable" desires. I also explore accusations of queerbaiting that were sometimes leveled against the show.

In chapter 3, "Stupid Word," I extend the focus on representation to *Killing Eve*'s portrayals of psychopaths. Drawing from critical disability studies, I analyze the series' twofold challenge to television narratives of monstrosity and to psychiatric classification and expertise.

In chapter 4, "Sorry to Disappoint," I shift from representation to audience reception, examining the widespread backlash against the series' controversial ending. I analyze the ending itself, then home in on allegations that *Killing Eve* used the "bury your gays" trope. The chapter addresses audience dynamics, industry conditions, and broader cultural and historical factors that influence contemporary television. I conclude with a short reflection on *Killing Eve*'s impact on popular culture, underscoring the series' status as culturally significant milestone TV.

1

CHIC AS SHIT

Style, Tone, and Genre

Killing Eve is a long-form serialized drama that tells its story across multiple seasons. As such, it exemplifies what Jason Mittell calls "complex TV."[1] As Mittell explains, complex TV emerged in the 1990s at the crossroads of multiple industry developments, including the rise of DVD and streaming technologies that displaced syndication as a central revenue source. These new modes of distribution allowed viewers to control the order in which they watched episodes, in turn enabling television stories to exceed episode bounds.

As a distinct form of storytelling, complex TV requires considerable investment from viewers, who must watch countless hours of sequential episodes across multiple seasons and, oftentimes, years. To build and sustain viewer engagement, creators utilize multiple techniques, developing distinctive audio, visual, and tonal identities that become synonymous with the show. *Killing Eve* took these techniques to new heights, winning multiple industry craft awards. In doing so, it not only captured viewers' attention, but also built an original foundation for its queer subversions of the thriller.

In this chapter, I examine the "building blocks" of *Killing Eve*. First,

I discuss the series' style, exploring how its soundtrack and visuals borrow from 1960s spy shows to create an escapist and timeless atmosphere. Second, I analyze *Killing Eve*'s characters in relation to cat-and-mouse thriller archetypes. Here, I focus on the series' sharp subversion of gender conventions, as well as its disappointing replication of racial norms. Finally, I discuss *Killing Eve*'s tone, considering how its unique blend of humor, cruelty, and tenderness anchors the show's fantastical leaps to "emotional truth."[2] Throughout, I argue that *Killing Eve* evokes and exceeds thriller history to create its distinctive brand of escapist, feminist, queer TV.

Spy Thriller Style

As television studies scholar Jeremy Butler explains, multiple elements constitute television style, including costumes, soundtrack, editing, set design, cinematography, and actor positioning.[3] Style is the "how" of television: It is the way that programs create their meanings, and the way that viewers learn how to watch. Style, for instance, tells viewers whether a scene is supposed to be funny or terrifying (or neither or both), by cueing affective and cognitive responses through music, lighting, camera work, and more. Although style is sometimes dismissed as surface adornment, it serves as viewers' first point of contact with a program and consequently is key to success. In *Killing Eve*—a series that centers the unlikely love story between a killer and the agent who chases her—style does essential work, guiding viewers to suspend reality and enjoy the show's amoral queer thrills.

To craft its permissive and pleasure-soaked style, *Killing Eve* drew from the escapism of 1960s spy television. Dozens of spy shows aired during the decade, including the *The Avengers*, *I-Spy*, *The Prisoner* (ITV, 1967–68), and *The Man from U.N.C.L.E.* (NBC, 1964–68). These shows were sleek and playful, eschewing the realism of later spy series for cool outfits, action-packed fight scenes, and fast-paced fun. *The Avengers* was particularly notable, featuring a dapper gentleman, John Steed, and the stylish woman who worked alongside him: first Cathy

Gale and then Emma Peel. Both women appeared as Steed's equal, but the young and modern Emma Peel stole the show, as a smart and fashionable sharp-shooting spy who often exceeded Steed's wit and skill.[4]

Sixties spy TV built on the commercial success of the first James Bond film, *Dr. No* (Young, 1962). The film and its many sequels were also rooted in fantasy, as Bond traveled the globe, sipping martinis, bedding women, and defeating archvillains along the way. The fantasy was an imperialist one, as Bond put various "exotic" others in their place. It also reduced women to playthings and prizes, as signaled by character names such as Honey Ryder and Pussy Galore. As numerous scholars have argued, spy fiction—Bond and beyond—exposes and soothes national anxieties, whether attached to nuclear threats, collapsing empires, Cold War anxieties, or global conspiracies of various kinds.[5] Some scholars have analyzed *Killing Eve* in similar terms, attending to its fantasies of eastern Europe and its representations of global travel in Brexit times.[6] Here, however, I'm far more interested in *Killing Eve*'s engagement with spy thriller style and its specific use of soundtrack, visuals, and costuming to create escapist, queer TV.

Killing Eve's soundtrack directly evokes the retro spy thriller. Curated by music supervisors Catherine Grieves and David Holmes, the award-winning soundtrack is offbeat and eclectic, featuring obscure 1960s girl groups, electronic torch songs, rock 'n' roll B-sides, and rare psychedelic tracks. Each episode also features several tracks from Holmes's band, Unloved, alongside an original score composed by Holmes and bandmate Keefus Ciancia. *Killing Eve*'s creators planned this soundworld early in the project's development, seeking deep and powerful women's vocals to match the show's narrative premise. Woodward Gentle, for instance, told me that she first gravitated to Beth Ditto, before falling for Unloved vocalist Jade Vincent's "otherworldly" voice. Blending the lush orchestration of classic film scores with electronic beats, 1960s pop, and vocal instrumentalism,

Unloved's sultry, melancholic sound became synonymous with the show, providing consistency across seasons, even as writers, directors, and producers changed.

When sourcing songs for the soundtrack, Holmes and Grieves sought tracks that were women led and rooted in countries where scenes were set, with preference for the commercially obscure. As a result, *Killing Eve* features a wide range of women artists, from 1960s French pop and yé-yé (Françoise Hardy, Brigitte Bardot), 1970s Australian psychedelic gospel (Sister Irene O'Connor), 1980s German New Wave (Carambolage), and 1980s UK garage pop (The Delmonas). Constantly shifting language and style, the series' soundtrack helps viewers keep track of the action, as it hops from city to city: London, Paris, Moscow, Berlin. It also gives *Killing Eve* a heady and timeless quality that is central to its escapist appeal. The final season even includes a track by Shirley Bassey, most famous for her James Bond theme songs, "Goldfinger" and "Diamonds Are Forever."

Although *Killing Eve* is steeped in retro sixties sounds, its soundtrack supports distinctly contemporary character development. In season 1, the music focuses on Villanelle, with dramatic tracks showcasing different parts of her psyche. These include the upbeat and playful "Roller Girl" by Anna Karina, the menacing "Durch dunkle Tannen" by Die Wilde Jagd, the Romani folk song "Les Yeux Noirs" by Sergeï Troganov, and the vampy and violent "Killer Shangri-Lah" by Pshycotic Beats. Featured in multiple ads and trailers, the latter became *Killing Eve*'s de facto theme song, mixing electronic beats, sixties pastiche, and playfully sinister lyrics: "I had to kill you / I'm really sorry / Was it so much fun?"

In contrast, Eve's early scenes are paired with a more subdued and melancholic sound, only to shift as her interest in Villanelle grows. This reaches a stunning climax in the season 1 finale, where Eve trashes Villanelle's apartment in cathartic fury to the raucous beats of "Ruckus Fracas," a drum-and-guitar-heavy track by Universal Music Productions. By season 2, Eve has earned her own dramatic soundtrack, including "Screw You" by Ramases and Selket and "She's My Witch" by the Fireflies. As music writer Leah Broad notes, music within complex TV helps viewers distinguish between essential and nonessential elements, directing them to the characters, scenes, and storylines that require closest attention. *Killing Eve*'s music makes it clear: Attend to Eve and Villanelle.[7]

Killing Eve's soundtrack also establishes Eve and Villanelle's queer dynamic as the show's central concern. Notably, viewers first learn that *Killing Eve* is a queer love story through its musical cues. In episode 2, for example, Eve meets with her soon-to-be boss, Carolyn Martens, to discuss female assassins, initiating a life-changing journey, rife with risk and deadly violence ("I'll Deal with Him Later," 1.2). The music that accompanies Eve, however, is slow and dreamy, laden with romantic longing, as conveyed in the lyrics: "I remember when I first noticed that you liked me back" (Cigarettes After Sex, "K"). Subsequent songs likewise evoke a romantic dynamic that subverts on-screen action, often in disorienting ways. For example, midway through season 1, Villanelle shoots at Eve's car on a country lane, attempting to assassinate a coworker hiding in the backseat ("I Have a Thing About Bathrooms," 1.5). When Eve exits the car to confront Villanelle, the stage is set for a terrifying showdown, only to be transformed into a lovers' lane meeting, as a haunting Unloved track voices the unlikely question that anchors the show: "If I gave you my heart, would you take it?" (Unloved, "Cry Baby Cry"). Woodward Gentle explained to me how David Holmes scored such scenes:

> Quite often I'd verbally pitch out a season and David would ask me: What are the locations? What are the dynamics? He got the vibe really, really well. It was thrilling because he didn't score for action. He scored for mood. We quite often tried to be counterintuitive. Normally when you'd have beating drums and rhythm and tension, we'd play a languorous, drawn-out, beautiful melody with Jade's incredible voice.

This emphasis on mood over action—and counterintuitive juxtapositions—was key to *Killing Eve*'s seductive style. As individual tracks infused the show with a timeless quality, often evoking earlier eras, their synchronization with unlikely scenes offered a fresh interpretive lens: romantic longing and queer desire. Pressed to juggle dissonant audio and visual inputs, viewers became more attentive to—and more invested in—Eve and Villanelle's bond.

Killing Eve's visual identity further reflects spy thriller iconography. Each episode opens in media res—in the midst of the action—eschewing the lengthy introductory sequences typical of most television dramas. It then cuts to designer Matt Willey's award-winning title card: KILLING EVE, spelled out in narrow sharp lettering, with a drop of blood descending from the inverted points. The custom-made typeface establishes *Killing Eve*'s ominous tone, while the blood drop hints at weaponry, in a subtle nod to James Bond's opening "gun-barrel" sequence, with its bullets and curtain of blood.

Killing Eve's filming locations and set designs also evoke classic spy thrillers, as Eve and Villanelle's cat-and-mouse chase unfolds across genre-typical European cities, announced by Willey's location cards.

 Killing Eve's distinctive title card, designed by Matt Willey.

One of *Killing Eve*'s location cards, designed by Matt Willey.

Unlike the functional black-and-white cards often used in television and film, *Killing Eve*'s location cards are an integral part of scene composition, appearing in a rotating palette of translucent lettering that float over each international locale: a cool blue for a Berlin highway, for instance, and a dusty pink for a Parisian street. The visual design heightens the show's viewing pleasures and reinforces *Killing Eve*'s distinctive style.

Killing Eve's lush visuals lay the groundwork for the series' queer pursuits, juxtaposing the opulence of the spy fantasy with the banality of Eve's life, to frame her attraction to Villanelle. Villanelle, for example, moves through Europe as a cosmopolitan Bond-style flaneur. Unconstrained by the realities of travel, she simply appears in new locations and traverses them with ease, riding on Berlin's U-Bahn or Paris's Métro, or motorbiking through Tuscany's hills. In contrast, Eve loses luggage, gets pushed around on underground platforms, and struggles to haul bags up hotel stairs. Similarly, the women's homes are a study in contrasts. Villanelle's Parisian apartment is light and spacious, styled with an eclectic mix of furniture and trinkets, a closet stuffed with designer clothes, a dresser loaded with perfumes, and a fridge filled with expensive champagne. Located in a grandiose and aged building, where peeling wallpaper only enhances its bohemian charms, it is a far cry from Eve's cozy and cluttered London home. When Carolyn asks Eve to describe Villanelle's apartment—after Eve has secretly trashed it—Eve retorts, "Chic as shit" ("Do You Know How to Dispose of a Body?," 2.1). The juxtaposition of Villanelle's luxuries and Eve's labors sets the stage for *Killing Eve*'s voyeuristic pleasures, as Eve's looking produces a longing that sows the seeds of a deeper desire.

While *Killing Eve*'s elegant title cards and stunning locations are central to its visual design, its costuming warrants particular attention. Mirroring its focus on setting, the series employs clothing to define and differentiate characters. Eve, for example, pays little attention to her appearance: She favors anoraks and high-street brands, and her clothes are often drab and disheveled. In contrast, Villanelle loves to dress up: peacock-like in her desire for attention, chameleon-like in her shifting looks. From designer dresses to dandified suits, silk kimonos to biker boots, her ever-rotating wardrobe is fun and extravagant, often with a subversive edge.

Killing Eve's use of costumes echoes the flair of 1960s spy TV, particularly the fashion-consciousness of Emma Peel, whose style evoked "swinging London" and drove *The Avengers*' popular appeal. During the sixties, UK fans could even buy lookalike clothing from "The Avengers" collections in high-street shops.[8] Fifty years later, Villanelle's wardrobe played a similar role in *Killing Eve*'s visual pleasures. Fashion websites featured guides on how to recreate her outfits, while *Vogue* and *Marie Claire* named *Killing Eve* one of television's most fashionable shows.[9] The series even influenced red-carpet fashions, with multiple actors attending the 2019 Academy Awards in Villanelle-inspired pink tulle dresses.

Unlike 1960s spy TV, however, *Killing Eve*'s costuming offers more than eye-catching outfits: It also gestures beneath the surface to reveal new character depths. For example, when Villanelle attends a

Villanelle wears an iconic Molly Goddard dress to a psychological assessment ("I'll Deal with Him Later," 1.2).

compulsory psychological assessment, she wears a flouncy pink Molly Goddard dress, paired with black Balenciaga boots. As described by costume designer Phoebe de Gay, the soon-to-be-iconic outfit conveys more than the character's love of fashion: It is "Villanelle putting up two middle fingers to the world."[10] Similarly, in season 2, when Villanelle is assigned to kill Eve, she arrives in a vintage black Alexander McQueen gown and mourning veil, capturing her love of dramatics, but also her sadness at the task. Throughout the series, Villanelle's theatricality provides a window onto her psyche, while shaping *Killing Eve*'s playful visual style.

Villanelle's costumes were also hailed as notably queer. Fashion magazines claimed her as a "queer fashion icon" and praised her "switchy queer style," which seamlessly moved between high femme aesthetics and queer masculinity.[11] The latter is introduced in season 1, when Villanelle wears a striking Dries Van Noten suit while stalking the streets of Berlin, before murdering Eve's friend Bill in a nightclub.

Villanelle wears a Dries Van Noten suit, paired with a scarf she has stolen from Eve, as Bill follows her in Berlin ("Don't I Know You?," 1.3).

Again, the outfit performs double duty, signaling Villanelle's queer aesthetic, while also supporting the episode's visual design, assuming a quasi-metallic sheen under the lighting of the nightclub that heightens the terror of the scene.

Throughout *Killing Eve*, Villanelle's masculine suits communicate her queer sexual confidence and interest in power, most notably during her encounters with Eve. In season 3's pivotal "bus kiss" episode, for example, she confronts Eve on a London bus, wearing a pinstripe Chalayan suit, paired with bespoke designer perfume, to signal her declared transformation from a "Roman centurion," hurt in battle, to an "emperor . . . powerful beyond measure" ("Meetings Have Biscuits," 3.3). Villanelle's outfits also can be camp and playful, as when she dresses as an upper-class college boy to accost Eve's husband in Oxford and taunt him about sex with his wife. In a costume inspired by *Brideshead Revisited*, Villanelle wears a vintage white shirt, high-waisted beige pants, and a cable-knit sweater draped over her shoulders, fueling the scene's outrageous queer energy, further enhanced by the soundtrack's lyrics: "May the best man win" (Unloved, "When a Woman Is Around").[12]

As the Oxford scene illustrates, costuming worked in conjunction with soundtrack and setting to create *Killing Eve*'s distinctive style. Within the series, style did heavy lifting, persuading viewers that killing and romance could coexist, and that Villanelle's murder of Bill, for instance, would not only spark a genre-typical cat-and-mouse chase, but also bring the women together in a strangely compelling death-infused dance. By channeling the retro cool of 1960s spy shows, the series created a lush and playful universe that was anchored in recognizable locations but slightly unmoored from reality and time. This highly stylized fictional space invited viewers to suspend real-world concerns about violence and morality and revel in taboo queer thrills.

Villanelle visits Oxford dressed as a character from *Brideshead Revisited* ("Smell Ya Later," 2.5).

Cat-and-Mouse Characters

While 1960s spy shows provided the template for *Killing Eve*'s style, the more suspenseful cat-and-mouse thriller birthed its characters and initial plot. As a time-tested narrative form, the cat-and-mouse chase has a long cinematic history, dating back to classic film noirs such as *The Maltese Falcon* (Huston, 1941) and *The Big Sleep* (Hawks, 1946). It has also been widely used in twenty-first-century complex TV, particularly within crime and spy thrillers. The signature chase takes various forms, but typically centers two protagonists, manipulative mind games, blurred morality, and life-or-death stakes. The familiar structure gave *Killing Eve* a blueprint to follow that made it easy for viewers to watch—and writers to subvert.

On the surface, *Killing Eve*'s erotically charged cat-and-mouse chase wasn't new. The cold-blooded killer and dogged investigator are well-established archetypes, as is the dynamic that develops between them. The duo finds out they're not so different from one another, as mutual interest spirals into obsession, begetting an intimacy tinged with lust. An undercurrent of sexual tension has driven multiple cat-and-mouse chases, whether between a female detective and male killer (e.g., *The Fall*), male detective and female killer (e.g., *Luther*), or two men (e.g., *Hannibal*, NBC, 2013–15). Until *Killing Eve*, however, cat-and-mouse chases always centered the violence of men, regardless of their gender casting.

Certainly, recent years have seen an increase in women leads, most typically as a beleaguered white woman cop who tracks a dangerous violent man. On English-language television, Jane Tennison of *Prime Suspect* (ITV, 1991–2006) pioneered this role, paving the way for characters like Catherine Cawood (*Happy Valley*), Robin Griffin (*Top of the Lake*), and Stella Gibson (*The Fall*). A significant body of Nordic noir crime dramas have also featured women leads, including Saga Norén in Sweden and Denmark's *Bron/Broen* (SVT1/DR1, 2011–18), Sarah Lund in Denmark's *Forbrydelsen* (DR1, 2007–12), Sofia Karppi in Finland's

Karppi (Yle TV2/Netflix, 2018–21), and Inger Johanne Vik in Sweden's *Modus* (TV4, 2015–17). Led by powerful and complex women, these series focus on men's violence and women's vulnerability, as well as the policing practices that shore up both.

Television shows that feature women killers are far less common. Occasionally, such characters appear in film, most typically as assassins or spies. Here, two archetypes dominate: the Asian "dragon lady" assassin who is sexually devious and devoid of emotion (e.g., O-Ren Ishii in *Kill Bill: Vol. 1*, Tarantino, 2003), and the tragic white femme fatale, who uses sex to ensnare her targets, but does the work against her will (e.g., Dominika Egorova in *Red Sparrow*, Lawrence, 2018). The French film *Nikita* (Besson, 1990) offered a more nuanced portrayal, with its protagonist already guilty of murder, before being recruited as an assassin. However, its US television remake, *La Femme Nikita* (USA Network, 1997–2001), redirected back to white victimhood, presenting the blonde and blue-eyed Nikita as falsely accused of the inciting crime.[13]

Before *Killing Eve*, television series rarely cast women as unrepentant psychopathic killers. Alice Morgan of BBC's *Luther* was a striking exception: a brilliant, violent, charismatic woman who murdered her parents at the start of the series and reveled in her genius at not getting caught. Across five seasons, Alice killed multiple times, often to help detective John Luther, with whom she developed a deeply obsessive and romantic bond. Her character bore a clear resemblance to Villanelle, particularly as she enticed Luther to accept his own murderous urges. *Luther* also disrupted the genre's whiteness by casting a Black British actor, Idris Elba, in the leading role.

Killing Eve borrowed from television's cat-and-mouse thrillers with self-awareness and sly glee. The show had a particularly strong resonance with *Luther*, and the two were sometimes marketed together. BBC America even created a mash-up video that imagined Villanelle and Alice as roommates. At the same time, *Killing Eve* broke from the pack by rerouting the cat-and-mouse chase through two women leads: a young, white, Russian assassin who seemed to "belong" in the genre, and a middle-aged Korean American intelligence agent who did not.

Waller-Bridge explained to me how she developed this concept from Luke Jennings's novellas: "Luke's original idea of a cat and mouse between two women was inspired. I loved the moodiness of the world he created—Eve's crumbled life and the cold luxury of Villanelle. It was an incredible place to jump from. . . . When writing the show, I could feel an electricity in Villanelle's coldness and a power in the pull between them. I knew I hadn't seen that before and it was just spine tingling to discover their dynamic."

As Waller-Bridge "jumped" from Jennings's foundation, she re-created the character landscape, replacing most of the men with women. As a result, women occupy most key roles in *Killing Eve*, not only the agent and the assassin, but also their bosses, handlers, and peers. Notably, many of these characters are middle-aged or older. For example, Waller-Bridge increased Eve's age from late twenties to early forties to deepen the character's internal struggles and stage an age gap with Villanelle. She also replaced Eve's boss, Simon, with a new character: Carolyn Martens, a "stone-cold badass" in her early sixties, who leads MI6's Russian desk ("Nice Face," 1.1). Later seasons also introduce Dasha Duzran, a former assassin and current handler who is planning retirement in her late sixties, and Hélène, a queer single mother in her forties and high-ranking member of the Twelve. Crucially, the show doesn't use its unique casting to give a new look to an old story, but to interrogate the workings of gender within the genre and to foreground a different set of concerns.[14]

For example, as I described in the introduction, *Killing Eve*'s opening scene parodies the genre convention of launching a thriller via a woman's corpse or scream. The device is pervasive. For instance, *The Killing* (AMC/Netflix, 2011–14) opens with a screaming woman running through the woods at night; *The Bridge* (SVT1/DR1, 2011–18) begins with a woman's body dumped on a bridge; and *Criminal Minds*

(CBS/Paramount, 2005–present) starts with a woman's abduction and punch to the face.[15] In interviews, Waller-Bridge described her desire to subvert the "screaming traumatized woman" trope—not only to deliver a surprising opening but also to critique the relentless brutalization of women on-screen. In response, critics praised *Killing Eve* as a welcome reprieve from the "masochism" of watching crime thrillers as a woman, and as "very entertaining payback for decades of dead girls wrapped in polythene in the woods."[16]

Killing Eve also subverts the familiar figure of the embattled lone woman cop. In part, this is because MI6 bosses within *Killing Eve* are almost all women, but it is also because Eve pursues Villanelle less as an agent and more as a fan. Eve's husband, Niko, points this out in season 1, shouting at Eve during an argument: "You're not saving the world, honeybunch. You're getting off on sniffing out a psycho." Eve is undeterred, however, brushing aside reminders of her broader mission and telling a Russian agent, for instance: "I don't give a shit about that. I just want the girls" ("Take Me to the Hole," 1.6).

As Eve pursues one "girl" in particular, *Killing Eve* moves beyond lone cop narratives to showcase a different site of struggle: Eve's battle with herself. This becomes clear in season 1's "breakthrough" scene, which doesn't focus on cracking the case, but breaking psychological barriers, literalized through shattering glass. The scene occurs midseason, as Eve waits for a bus, then notices a crack in the bus shelter glass. Inexplicably drawn to the rupture, Eve presses and prods with her finger, before using her elbow to smash the pane, only to appear stunned as it breaks. The scene captures core elements of Eve's character: intrigued, determined, impulsive, aroused, and acting without thought of consequence. It also hints at complex erotics (discussed in the next chapter), where shattering can be sexual and violent, both rooted in a desire to know.

Finally, *Killing Eve* challenges on-screen depictions of women assassins, albeit in more uneven ways. On the one hand, Villanelle fits genre conventions as a conventionally attractive, young, white, Russian

Eve presses at a crack in the glass until it shatters ("I Have a Thing About Bathrooms," 1.5).

woman. On the other, she doesn't use sex to do her job, breaking with femme-fatale archetypes. To highlight this shift, *Killing Eve* grants Villanelle self-awareness of the cultural expectations surrounding her role. In one scene, for example, Villanelle explains to Konstantin how she escaped a tricky situation:

VILLANELLE: I didn't want to tell you this part of the story because I knew you would be jealous.
KONSTANTIN: Hmm?
VILLANELLE: I had to use my tits.
KONSTANTIN: [*laughs*] To kill him? You killed him with your tits?

Although the scene is played for laughs, it draws attention to genre conventions that reduce women assassins to their bodies, particularly their breasts ("I Have a Thing About Bathrooms," 1.5). Notably, the only character who embraces the femme fatale trope is Carolyn, who fondly reminisces about suspicion-laced sex with Russian men during her former espionage days. Her recollections not only offer a rare portrayal of older women expressing sexual agency on television. They also signal the trope's datedness, contained in a memory of times gone by.

By exposing and rejecting genre tropes, *Killing Eve* creates space for women's bodies to be present in new ways. For example, *Killing Eve* pays scant attention to crime scene clues and investigations, instead exploring women's hunger, broadly defined, and often literalized through food. Key scenes are set in kitchens, and frequent references to consumption evoke destruction and desire. Smells also feature prominently, with perfume doubling as a weapon and mode of seduction, and Eve's interest in "sniffing out" Villanelle steeped in sexual overtones. Key dialogue signals these themes, as when Villanelle says, "Smell me, Eve," during a fight on a London bus ("Meetings Have Biscuits," 3.3), or when Eve remarks, "We would consume each other before we got old," during a shared ballroom dance ("Are You Leading or Am I?," 3.8). Episode titles also reflect these sensual interests—"The Hungry Caterpillar" (2.3), "Don't Get Eaten" (4.2), "Smell Ya Later" (2.5)—while song lyrics from season 4's trailer drive the point home: "I hunger for your love" (Righteous Brothers, "Unchained Melody").

Alongside its queer sensuality, *Killing Eve* foregrounds mundane aspects of women's embodiment that are rarely acknowledged within the thriller genre. For example, the series includes multiple references to menstruation: Villanelle keeps tampons alongside her bullets, speaks of having a heavy period, and uses a tampon to gain access to one of her targets, a move that Eve parallels in season 4. Similarly, when Villanelle returns a suitcase she's stolen from Eve (see chapter 2), she only includes one of Eve's items: a tube of yeast infection cream. This attentiveness to women's bodies, by other women, creates new possibilities within the thriller, blurring the lines between intimacy, intrusion, manipulation, and care. Such moves are far less feasible in shows that center the violence of men and they set the stage for *Killing Eve*'s exploration of women's queer desires.

Killing Eve opened the door to also tackle the genre's racial tropes, by casting Korean Canadian actor Sandra Oh as Eve. As signaled above, crime and spy thrillers are steeped in whiteness, with Asian women often excluded or confined to stereotypical dragon-lady roles. Although *Luther* made strides by featuring a Black man as its lead detective, no televised cat-and-mouse thriller before *Killing Eve* had featured a woman of color in the investigative role.

In the transition from book to screen, Eve's character underwent significant changes, from a white British woman in her late twenties to a Korean American woman in her early forties. The increase in age reflected an early creative decision (discussed above), while the switch in nationality happened later, when BBC America required an American to be cast in a leading role. The change in Eve's race came later still, when casting directors Suzanne Crowley and Gilly Poole selected Sandra Oh for the part. In early interviews, Oh praised the show's colorblind casting, noting that book-to-screen adaptations frequently switch characters' races, although this typically bends toward whiteness and rarely considers actors of color for roles originally written as white. The promise of this approach, however, ultimately fell short, as multiple scholars, critics, and fans have observed.[17]

Certainly, as a Korean American lead, Eve's presence in *Killing Eve* disrupts business as usual. Her racialized physical presence in spaces like MI6 meetings, government safe houses, and investigation rooms brings the genre's normative whiteness into sharp relief. Eve's race also adds dimensionality to her relationship with Villanelle, holding particular significance for queer Asian viewers. Eve's character is deeply complex and largely free of the stereotypical traits that accompany Asian women on television. Many early reviewers praised *Killing Eve*'s colorblind casting as progressive, contributing to its reputation as a groundbreaking show. As the series unfolded, however, its limited approach to racial representation became apparent.

Rooted in colorblind casting, *Killing Eve* adopts a race-neutral writing strategy that features a relatively diverse cast but rarely addresses race in the scripts. Most notably, the show pays scant attention to Eve's Korean American identity, denying her Korean family, friends, language, food, or even spoken acknowledgments of race. Instead, Eve appears on-screen as an "everywoman" who just happens to be Korean American, rather than a fully realized Korean American character. Woodward Gentle confirmed to me that *Killing Eve* had taken this approach, focusing on the depths of Eve's psyche, but not her cultural identity or ties.

This omission becomes more striking when contrasted with the series' attention to white characters' cultural identities. Eve's husband, Niko, is Polish, for instance, and in early episodes, Eve attends his Polish bridge club, asks him to translate witness testimony, and even speaks a few words of Polish herself—a full season before she speaks Korean, and two seasons before she engages with London's Korean community. Similarly, Villanelle's Russian identity is omnipresent. She spends significant time in the country, and Russian people populate her life. *Killing Eve* even explores the cultural roots of its white characters as Niko, Villanelle, and Carolyn (via a flashback episode) spend time in Polish, Russian, and German homes.

Killing Eve centers whiteness in subtle ways, too. Virtually all characters of color are romantically or sexually paired with white people: Eve (with Niko, Villanelle, Hugo, and Hélène); Elena (with Kenny); May (with Villanelle); and Pam (with Darren).[18] Additionally, *Killing Eve*'s vast and eclectic soundtrack does not include South Korean tracks, despite using Russian songs for Villanelle's and Konstantin's scenes. This is particularly striking, since multiple 1960s Korean girl groups had crossover American appeal, offering both a sound and identity that would have matched the show's style. The series' humor also sometimes rubs up against racial stereotypes, as when Villanelle treats Eve as her maid ("You're Mine," 2.8), or wedding participants mistake Eve to be Japanese ("Hello Losers," 4.8). As media scholar Kristen Warner notes, television shows that accrue a diverse set of characters through colorblind casting can inadvertently reproduce racial stereotypes by glossing over the political histories that give meaning to actions on-screen.[19]

Finally, *Killing Eve* does not interrogate the role of whiteness within the genre, despite its centrality to spy and assassin storylines. For example, Villanelle's race is integral to her work, enabling her easy movement through the spaces where she enacts her kills: the white-dominated garden party, the political fundraiser, and the corporate office, for instance. *Killing Eve* does not attend to this, even as its pairing of a Korean American agent and white assassin establishes prime conditions to do so. For example, in one early scene, Eve reels off a long list of characteristics that likely inform Villanelle's success: her gender, youth, intelligence, flair, linguistic ability, and psychopathy, but, strikingly, not her race ("I'll Deal with Him Later," 1.2). By shying away from naming whiteness, *Killing Eve* perpetuates a pattern of racial avoidance that inadvertently reproduces the taken-for-granted dominance of whiteness on-screen.

Certainly, there are brief exceptions. Most notably, at the start of season 3, Eve appears in New Malden, London's largest Korean neighborhood, shopping at a Korean supermarket and working in a Korean restaurant kitchen, while recovering from a gunshot wound. In these scenes, Eve is surrounded by the cultural signifiers previously absent from the show: food, language, implied family, even a Korean drama on TV that depicts a shooting, transplanting Eve and Villanelle's recent storyline to a popular Korean cultural context. The promise of these scenes, however, is short-lived. As soon as Carolyn arrives at the restaurant, Eve reorients toward white characters and her Korean roots are not broached again.

Criticisms of *Killing Eve*'s approach to race reached a peak in 2020, when one of the season 4 writers (Kayleigh Llewellyn) shared a screenshot of the Zoom writers' room on social media, depicting an exclusively white group. Sid Gentle Films had appointed two writers of color, one of whom worked on season 4 (Isis Davis), but nonetheless the screenshot accurately captured a predominantly white creative team. Although creators of color have also engaged in colorblind casting and race-neutral writing—most notably Shonda

Eve works in the kitchen of a Korean restaurant in New Malden ("Slowly Slowly Catchy Monkey," 3.1).

Rhimes—decisions to omit race carry additional weight within white-led productions, particularly when those productions aim to disrupt television tropes that reflect and perpetuate social inequalities.[20] Undoubtedly, *Killing Eve* broke new ground when casting Eve, and the character's on-screen presence brought the whiteness of the genre into sharp relief. At the same time, the show missed a valuable opportunity to integrate challenges to white dominance into the heart of the show.

Bloody Funny

Alongside its engagements with spy-thriller style and cat-and-mouse conventions, *Killing Eve* cultivated a distinctive tone that shaped viewers' experiences of on-screen events. This tone was defined by a series of juxtapositions: comedy and drama, suspense and mundanity, violence and tenderness, and fantasy and "emotional truth." Each season's head writer approached these juxtapositions in distinct ways, yet season 1 established a tonal template that endured throughout the series.

Within *Killing Eve*, tone did significant work, tethering the series' outlandish thrills to psychological nuance and depth. At its core, *Killing Eve* was darkly comedic, driven by Waller-Bridge's wicked humor and signature wit. The comedy marked a sharp departure from Jennings's novellas, as well as the genre as a whole. It also broke from earlier feminist interventions into crime thriller television. For example, series such as *The Killing* and *Happy Valley* expanded the genre's emotional and thematic scope by emphasizing the devastating costs of violence. In doing so, they adopted a serious and somber tone in line with much prestige television. In sharp contrast, *Killing Eve* amplified and exaggerated violence to the point of absurdity, almost always committed by women, and stripped of consequence or care. The series' irreverent and mischievous tone represented a bold innovation within the thriller, opening up new possibilities for feminist storytelling on television.

Certainly, other thrillers have used humor for genre play. *Hannibal*, for instance, framed its cannibalistic killer as a refined food snob who hosted elegant dinner parties, while *You* (Lifetime/Netflix, 2018–25) blended the serial killer narrative with romantic comedy, exposing the pathology of both. The humor in those shows, however, was understated, operating as a sly nod to those in the know. In contrast, *Killing Eve*'s humor was front and center, as captured in one of its early print advertisements—a black page punctuated by two words: BLOODY. FUNNY.

Humor plays a vital role in *Killing Eve*. Waller-Bridge explained to me how she used comedy to bring the series to life:

> It's important to me that all the characters have a different sense of humor and different boundaries when it comes to being shocked or moved by something. That way they're all just bumping into each other all the time, trying to read each other and getting it

> wrong. If the characters all share the same sort of humor or tone it will start to feel flat. Allowing one character to surprise the other is when it comes to life and if I'm not getting surprised myself, I know something's gone wrong.

Exchanges between Carolyn and Eve exemplify this dynamic. When the two travel to Russia, for instance, Carolyn references a "tit for tat" prisoner exchange, only for Eve to joke about "tit" and Carolyn to not understand ("Take Me to the Hole," 1.6). Such scenes are funny, of course, but they also capture the awkwardness of misunderstandings in social interaction, grounding the show's escapist fantasy in an emotionally resonant core.

Villanelle's humor does similar work. In deciding how to "humanize" Villanelle, Waller-Bridge gave her a sense of humor, in sharp contrast to earlier spy shows that built empathy for women assassins through tragic backstories, as in *La Femme Nikita* and *Red Sparrow*. As a result, Villanelle wins viewers' hearts with childlike mischief. In one scene, she stuffs a dead fly into a muffin for an unsuspecting woman to eat. In another, she sneaks into Eve's home just to use her toothbrush, hide her mail, and mess up her CD collection. Villanelle's deadpan wit further enhances her dangerous charm. When Eve confronts her—"I have lost two jobs, a husband, and a best friend because of you"—Villanelle shoots back, "Yeah, but you got some really nice clothes out of it" ("God, I'm Tired," 1.8). In another scene, when Konstantin chastises her for shooting him, Villanelle shrugs: "You're not still mad about that?" ("The Hungry Caterpillar," 2.3). Villanelle's humor both underscores and undercuts her psychopathy, disarming viewers who know they should recoil from her coldness but lean in closer for hints of warmth.

Killing Eve's juxtaposition of theatrical violence and domesticity similarly grounds the show. In the pilot episode, Eve narrates a gruesome fantasy of murdering her husband only to pivot to plans for supper. Similarly, Villanelle's later intrusion into Eve's home is

Wearing the dress that Villanelle sent her, Eve defends herself with a toilet brush when Villanelle breaks into her house ("I Have a Thing About Bathrooms," 1.5).

undercut by Eve's defensive weapon of choice: a toilet brush. These humorous scenes remind viewers that *Killing Eve*'s violence is fantastical, while simultaneously binding the fantasy to the mundane objects of everyday life.

Waller-Bridge explained to me how *Killing Eve*'s tone emerged organically from her conceptualization of the characters:

> In the spy genre it's easy to get Very Serious, but if the characters are flawed and desperate—as I believe all good ones are—that tone should bubble up naturally. I also wanted people to have a good time watching these characters. It's fantasy after all. I remember knowing the tone for sure when writing the scene in the bathroom in episode five. Villanelle breaks into Eve's house for a conversation, but Eve freaks out and locks herself in the bathroom all culminating in Eve using a loo brush as a weapon. That was an aahh

moment. It felt true—there was nothing else in there and it IS disgusting, it was funny, but it was also desperate. Bingo!

Waller-Bridges's belief in the primacy of "flawed and desperate" characters drives *Killing Eve*'s raw energy, enticing viewers to root for its women even as they do terrible things, tearing themselves and others apart. It also makes the characters relatable. *Killing Eve* may not be narratively probable, but it feels surprisingly true.

Finally, *Killing Eve* juxtaposes humor and pathos to stage its drama in unexpected ways. Villanelle's jokes, for instance, sometimes signal an interest in closeness that otherwise might remain unspoken. In season 1's finale, Eve confronts Villanelle in her flat:

EVE: What do you want? Honestly. Don't be a dick.

VILLANELLE: Normal stuff. A nice life. Cool flat. Fun job. Someone to watch movies with.

As Villanelle speaks, the moment teeters between irony and vulnerability. An assassin seeking "normal stuff" and a "fun job" sounds comedic, but her interest in "someone to watch movies with" feels sincere, surprising viewers, as well as Eve, and possibly Villanelle herself ("God, I'm Tired," 1.8). In such moments of tonal ambiguity, *Killing Eve*'s escapist fun takes on new emotional weight, as parody and earnestness blend, leaving viewers to ponder the longing beneath the laughs.

When writing *Fleabag* several years prior, Waller-Bridge crafted dialogue that similarly interwove comedy and drama to explore loneliness and grief. In interviews, she explained the ways she used humor strategically, so as to "punch viewers in the gut with the drama" once their guard was down.[21] In *Killing Eve*, that punch could be literal, as when Eve stabs Villanelle in the stomach moments after the above exchange. The dizzying sequence of affects and actions came to define

Killing Eve, which ricocheted from teasing to tender to violent to funny and back again throughout the show.

I asked Waller-Bridge about the appeal of *Killing Eve*'s tone, particularly its distinct combination of humor, cruelty, and tenderness:

> I think I see the world in that tone! There is so much comedy and heartbreak happening around us all the time. A shy person offering a cup of tea to a room full of people and no-one noticing can be funny and devastating. I suppose I look for surprise and contradiction and a psychopath killer just wanting to watch a movie with the agent who is after her was an absolute bullseye for me. . . . I saw the whole show as a love story so that helped with the co-existence of tenderness and cruelty, which are requirements for any truly epic tales of romance.

As Waller-Bridge explained, *Killing Eve*'s tone provided a way to conjure a world layered with complex, competing emotions. In that world, hope and heartbreak went hand in hand, tying the show's escapist fantasy to a reality that many viewers felt as their own. This tonal richness worked in tandem with *Killing Eve*'s style and genre subversions to create an off-kilter world, where murder could double as seduction, without triggering viewers' moral qualms, yet still feel emotionally true. In doing so, it laid the foundation for Eve and Villanelle's "epic" romance and mobilized the series' groundbreaking portrayals of queer desire, as I now explore.

2

DEFINE RELATIONSHIP

Expanding Queer Representation

Killing Eve's distinctive style, subversive characters, and audacious tone not only revitalized the thriller genre, but also opened new pathways for queer women's television. Most strikingly, the series offered a rich meditation on queer desire, expanding the ways it might be envisioned, the sites in which it could emerge, and techniques for bringing it into view.

In this chapter, I explore those innovations. First, I discuss the series' queer content, focusing on its detachment of sexual desire from identity and its emphasis on kink dynamics. Second, I turn to issues of craft, exploring the show's appropriation of genre conventions and use of form to communicate "unsayable" desires. Finally, I analyze accusations of queerbaiting that were sometimes leveled at the show. While previous scholars have used Lacanian psychoanalytic frameworks to analyze *Killing Eve*'s queer representations, I take a more grounded approach to situate these representations within the history of queer women on television.[1]

Admittedly, it is a fairly brief history. Prior to the 1990s, UK and US television paid little attention to romantic or sexual intimacy between women. Exceptions include *Girl*, a short drama that aired in 1974, depicting a secret relationship and on-screen kiss between two women (*Second City Firsts*, BBC, 1973–78); *The Golden Girls* (NBC, 1985–92), which featured a single-episode storyline in 1986; and *Hill Street Blues* (NBC, 1981–87), which introduced a recurring lesbian character that same year.

In the 1990s, representation became more frequent, often taking the form of one-off "lesbian kiss episodes" in hit shows such as *L.A. Law* (NBC, 1986–94), *Rosanne* (ABC, 1988–97), and *Ally McBeal* (Fox, 1997–2002). These kisses were typically included as novelty scenes designed to drive ratings, rather than contribute to meaningful character or story arcs. Nevertheless, *Friends* (NBC, 1994–2004) and *Ellen* (ABC, 1994–98) offered more significant inclusion, while *Emmerdale* (ITV, 1972–present) and *Brookside* (Channel 4, 1982–2003) became the first UK soap operas to feature lesbian characters and storylines. The late 1990s also witnessed landmark representation in *Bad Girls* (ITV, 1999–2006), a UK prison drama that included multiple lesbian relationships, and *Buffy the Vampire Slayer* (The WB/UPN, 1997–2003), a teen-oriented supernatural drama that featured the first regular lesbian character on US television.[2]

The following decade, *The L Word* (Showtime, 2004–9) continued to break new ground as a "lesbian soap drama" set in Los Angeles that featured an ensemble cast of upper-middle-class lesbians and bisexuals, the first of its kind for primetime television. *The L Word's* success laid the foundation for subsequent shows that drastically increased visibility in the 2010s. From long-running soaps like *Coronation Street* (ITV, 1960–present), to new teen shows like *Skins* (E4, 2007–13) and *Glee* (Fox, 2009–15), to US dramas like *Grey's Anatomy* (ABC, 2005–present) and *The Good Wife* (CBS, 2009–16), lesbians and bisexual women appeared on television at unprecedented rates.

As Kate McNicholas Smith explains, however, this increased visibility was accompanied by greater conformity. Characters were often styled according to heteronormative codes of femininity and pursued traditional goals of monogamous romance, marriage, and motherhood. Storylines frequently followed a familiar coming-out trajectory, tracing a journey from shame to pride that required identity to be voiced in socially sanctioned ways. As Suzanna Danuta Walters argues, these representations reflected broader assimilationist trends that sought LGBTQ+ inclusion by erasing distinctively queer cultures, identities, and desires.[3]

Certainly, there were important exceptions. For example, *Orange Is the New Black* (Netflix, 2013–19) included butch and trans women characters who better reflected the gender diversity of LGBTQ+ communities. It also featured working-class, Black, and Latina characters at higher rates than previous shows. Nonetheless, as McNicholas Smith demonstrates, such series were exceptions. During the 2010s, television representation was shaped by a new "lesbian normal," with conformity as its price.

Killing Eve premiered against this backdrop, delivering its own playful and subversive twist on normalized television narratives. In doing so, it helped propel a new wave of queer women's TV. As Thomas Brassington, Debra Ferreday, and Dany Girard argue, the turn-of-the-decade ushered in a fresh slate of shows that brought queerness into the mainstream without capitulating to cisheteropatriarchal norms, as seen in *Vida* and *Work in Progress* (Showtime, 2019–21), for instance.[4] At the forefront of this shift, *Killing Eve* set aside the "lesbian normal" to depict queer women's sexualities in more complex and compelling ways.

In describing *Killing Eve* as "queer," I use the term in specific ways—first, as an umbrella term for LGBTQ+ identities, aligning with popular cultural usage. I describe Villanelle as queer, for instance, to avoid rigid distinctions between lesbian and bisexual identities, or the need to interpret her infrequent sexual encounters with men. Second, and more specifically, I use the term to denote nonnormative fluid sexualities that are unattached to identity concerns. This definition is widely used in the field of queer studies, and it proves particularly useful when analyzing *Killing Eve*. Finally, I use "queer" to describe a critical method that uncovers the homoerotics of cultural phenomena that are not overtly about sex. Specifically, I argue that *Killing Eve* "queers" the cat-and-mouse thriller by using the genre's tropes, props, and settings to spotlight its latent same-gender desires.[5]

Queer Content

Killing Eve is set in a fundamentally queer universe where same-gender desires are ubiquitous. Villanelle is the central queer character, regularly engaging in hookups, flirtations, and threesomes with women. Her sexual history also includes long-term relationships, most notably with a prison girlfriend (Nadia) and a teacher during her adolescence (Anna). She even has a wife (Maria), although the marriage ends abruptly when their wedding reception devolves into a chaotic brawl. Villanelle has sex with a man (Sebastian) early in season 1, after Konstantin encourages her to do something "normal," but her subsequent sex life centers on women, and her fantasies home in on Eve.

Killing Eve also features a wide array of supporting queer characters. These include Eve's friend Bill; several assassins (Felix, Gunn, Nadia); high-ranking officials within the Twelve and MI6 (Hélène, Paul); a vicar's daughter (May); and multiple partners, flings, and exes (Anna, Pamela, Maria, Fernanda). Same-gender desires are also referenced in conversation, including those that verge on taboo. Carolyn, for instance, explains to Eve why her father used to frequent the bathing ponds of a London park: "Very popular in the fifties with spies. Ideal place for a sensitive conversation. And to have sex with boys, of course, which would have been an added bonus for Daddy" ("Do You Know How to Dispose of a Body?," 2.1). Unlike previous shows that required queer characters to assimilate into a heteronormative world, *Killing Eve* flips the script by rewriting the world as deeply queer.

Despite centering a wide range of same-gender desires and relationships, *Killing Eve* has little interest in sexual identity. An early exchange sets the tone, when Eve learns that Bill—a man in his sixties, married to a woman—has had extensive sexual experiences with men. When Eve asks if he is gay, Bill casually shrugs. "I just fall in love with whoever I fall in love with," he replies ("Don't I Know You?," 1.3). Bill's disinterest in sexual identity, combined with his ease in describing sex with "hundreds" of men and his familiarity with queer culture, points toward a distinctive approach to queer representation that guides the series as a whole.

Bracketing questions of identity, *Killing Eve* dives deep into the complexity of desire, specifically between Eve and Villanelle. As Waller-Bridge explained to me:

> I didn't want either woman to be ashamed of her desire. Confused, intrigued, frightened of it absolutely but I was so much more excited by the complexity of their attraction than the identity of it. Eve's pull towards Villanelle was a surprise to her and totally intoxicating. She both worshipped and reviled this exquisite murderer. Villanelle is beautiful, of course, but she is also living an outrageous life, rejecting the inexplicably guilt-ridden, apologetic version of modern female existence that Eve had adopted. She broke all the rules and Eve wanted to be near that.

By putting aside the shame/pride binary that often organizes media narratives of same-gender attraction, *Killing Eve* stages desire in its full, messy complexity, laced with contradictory emotions: intrigue, fear, confusion, surprise. Eve's attraction to a literal murderer also makes room for desire to be conflicted and ambivalent, without the shadow of homophobia. In this way, the series' fun and fantastical premise enables its deeper theme: the life-changing force of complex, illogical, embodied desire.

Killing Eve also explores same-gender desire in unusually expansive ways. As Waller-Bridge indicated, Eve's attraction is not only driven by Villanelle's beauty, but by the freedom she represents. This approach does not deny Eve's erotic pull but stretches the idea of the erotic itself. Waller-Bridge elaborated when describing Villanelle's attraction to Eve:

> For Villanelle, aside from the overt physical attraction she had for Eve, she was also basking in Eve's attention. She loved being hunted, could feel she was being obsessed over and she liked it. Villanelle's job required her to go unnoticed, which was painful for a woman who considered herself so extraordinary. Suddenly someone was fixated on her, studying her, acknowledging her skill, trying to catch her . . . which is very sexy to her. I think desire, when really explored, is often so much more to do with the self than the object. I got to really explore that with these two.

Killing Eve's expansive exploration of women's same-gender desires is rare on television, where those desires are often reduced to indicators of identity or subsumed within conventional romantic arcs. Without those familiar organizing forces, *Killing Eve* opens space for new formulations: desire entangled with impulse and fantasy; desire exceeding logic and reason; desire that hits like a ton of bricks.

Killing Eve does more than center longing, however. It also foregrounds kink dynamics that are stunning to see on mainstream television. In recent years, kink has become the preferred term for a wide range of nonnormative sexual practices, including sadism, masochism, dominance, submission, exhibitionism, voyeurism, fetishism, and more. Within *Killing Eve*, these dynamics not only drive Eve and Villanelle's relationship but permeate the series' fictional world. Throughout the show, characters talk about BDSM practices, cultures, and venues as unremarkable parts of their sex lives, while jokes about "safe words" straddle the worlds of kink and MI6 surveillance. Woodward Gentle explained to me how kink assumed its central role: "A lot of it came from Phoebe's lead that was picked up by Emerald. We had a room full of women that just naturally lent into it. There's a conversation in Germany before Bill dies about kink and how you just happen to love who you love. That was just the world of *Killing Eve*." Like its approach to same-gender attractions, *Killing Eve* normalizes kink by adapting the world to conform to its characters, rather than the other way around.

Killing Eve's depictions of kink also break from thriller conventions that often rely on sadism, bondage, and voyeurism to "spice up" scenes of sexual violence. As Woodward Gentle explained, she aimed to avoid the genre cliché where psychopathic killers, typically men, derive sexual pleasure from murdering women:

> I was fed up with seeing labeled psychopathic killers getting a huge sexual hit from killing. I think it's a cheap trick within television. With Villanelle, it was more like, "I can do this and I'm really good at it, and it's gonna give me whatever hit I want." Quite often television does that to bring in an audience and I didn't want this to be a show for men to get off on. I think it's much more interesting to explore sex and kinks separately from killing. What's really interesting is the sexual charge that goes on in the gaps.

To support this fresh approach, *Killing Eve* emphasizes sexual consent from the outset. The pilot introduces the framework when Villanelle tells a mafia boss who tries to fondle her, "You really should ask before you touch a person," before jamming a hairpin into his eye ("Nice Face," 1.1). The juxtaposition of Villanelle's lesson on consent and her lethal violence is disorienting and comedic, yet it also reveals the show's sexual politics: Within this fictional universe, sexual violence will not be indulged. This not only challenges the routinization of sexual violence on television. It also clears the ground for kink to play a far more interesting narrative role.

The series introduces its approach to kink early in season 1, when Villanelle kills a man at a Berlin fetish clinic ("Don't I Know You?," 1.3). Initially, the episode treads familiar ground, linking the psychopathic killer to sexual deviance, as Villanelle straps the man to a gurney, clamps his testicles, and gasses him to death. When Eve and Bill arrive to investigate, however, the episode takes a startling turn. Until that point, Bill has appeared in the series as a presumptively heterosexual man. Once in Berlin, however, his personal experiences with queer kink practices come into view, as he flirts with an old male friend, reminisces about wild nights at the Glitter Morgue nightclub, and lectures a Chinese official about the pleasures and etiquette of consensual spanking. Shocked and slightly titillated, Eve asks Bill how he knows about "that kink stuff," only for Bill to smile and reply that he had previously lived in Berlin for eight years and "said yes to everything for five." The episode plays a pivotal role within the series, as Villanelle murders Bill in the final minutes, setting in motion her mutually obsessive dynamic with Eve. Bill's role in the series, however, does more than catapult the women together. It also offers a lens through which to view their collision: one of kinky queer desire.

Throughout *Killing Eve*, Eve and Villanelle's relationship is infused with perverse impulses and interactions that upend television norms. Although the women don't share a romantic kiss until the series' finale, they take clear and consistent sexual pleasure in one another, through voyeurism and exhibitionism, shared masturbation, sex with substitutes, power play, and the sadomasochist pleasures of causing and receiving pain. Villanelle, for example, communicates her interest in Eve through love notes that she leaves at crime scenes, and gifts laden with sex and violence: decadent clothing to apologize for murder, lipstick concealing a hidden blade, and flowers arranged to spell "Eve" in the style of a funeral bouquet. Villanelle also watches Eve from a distance, and fantasizes about her during sex, even dressing another woman in Eve's clothing and calling her by Eve's name. Waller-Bridge explained to me the appeal of integrating kink into *Killing Eve*:

> Kink has so much to do with self-acceptance and trust. To know what you like and to be able to ask for it is so far from what Eve can

> articulate for herself. She is excited and moved by Bill sharing his sexual preferences with her, which only encourages her to question her own boundaries and desires. Villanelle however explores her kinks so openly and what a joy that is to write! Sex is boring and functional for Villanelle until she starts integrating Eve into her fantasies . . . a really fun way to play with the character's inner life. I also believe everyone is essentially kinky on some level, but so often too vulnerable to talk about it, so everyone leans in when that conversation comes up.

By treating kink as a common but stigmatized sexual interest, *Killing Eve* expands both the range of desires depicted on television and the ways in which they are understood. Moreover, it forges a new creative path by mobilizing sexual fantasy as a device for illuminating characters' inner worlds.

Kink plays a particularly key role in Eve's character development in season 2. Written by Emerald Fennell, the season explores Eve's growing erotic agency and deepening investment in the attention she garners from Villanelle. For example, her eager reception of Villanelle's gifts transforms their meaning from threat to seduction, positioning herself as an equal match in their dangerous game. Most strikingly, when Eve discovers the tube of lipstick that Villanelle has slipped into her handbag, she applies it at home, cutting herself on its hidden blade. Rather than recoil in terror, Eve smiles into the bathroom mirror, caressing the bloody wound, intrigued. Eve also fantasizes about Villanelle during sex with others, even using an MI6 surveillance earpiece to listen to Villanelle masturbate for her, as she initiates sex with a colleague during a mission in Rome ("Wide Awake," 2.7). Eve's kinky desires primarily center on Villanelle, but they sometimes extend to other people. In one scene, for instance, Eve's husband pins her against the wall and demands to know whether she wants to be loved or frightened. Clearly aroused, Eve replies "I don't know," before crawling to bed on her hands and knees ("I Hope

Eve cuts her lip on a blade that Villanelle has hidden in a tube of lipstick ("The Hungry Caterpillar," 2.3).

You Like Missionary!," 2.6). Later that season, when Eve learns that a man she meets at a high-security psychiatric hospital has killed three women, she retorts: "He could kill the shit out of me" ("Wide Awake," 2.7). Eve's fascination with power play also attaches to Villanelle's boss, Hélène, in a season 4 scene that parodies a first dinner date: Eve cuts her finger while chopping vegetables, Hélène sucks blood from the wound, and the women exchange mock pleasantries—"I like holidays, dogs, long walks on the beach"—while Hélène burns Eve's hand on the stove in a form of torture that Eve later identifies as sexual ("Don't Get Eaten," 4.2).

Killing Eve's attentiveness to women's power-laden, perverse desires is unusual for television but aligns with key concepts from queer studies that illuminate the show's innovative work. For example, queer studies scholars conceptualize the relationship between sexual desire and identity to be a cultural construct rather than an inevitable fact.

This scholarship doesn't question the validity of same-gender desires but demonstrates that their meanings vary across time and place. As such, it emphasizes that sexual desire and sexual identity are distinct phenomena, each warranting attention in its own right.[6]

When focusing on sexual desire, queer theorists also differentiate between object choice and sexual aim. "Object choice" refers to the person or thing a person desires (e.g., women, older people, animals), while "sexual aim" refers to behaviors that give a person sexual pleasure (e.g., voyeurism, sadism, kissing). In contemporary western societies, sexual identities are organized around the gender of object choice, such that a person identifies as lesbian, gay, bisexual, or heterosexual based on the gender they sexually desire. Gender, however, is not a salient characteristic of attraction for some people, and it can be overshadowed by alternate factors such as age. Additionally, sexual desire need not focus on object choice at all, but can center on sexual aim. For example, a person who enjoys exhibitionism or masochism may not be driven by characteristics of their partner(s), as much as by the pleasure and power of the exchange. Despite these variations, most cultural discussions of sexual difference are limited to the identities structured by gender and object choice (lesbian, gay, bisexual, heterosexual) and rarely acknowledge the myriad additional ways that desire can be lived and felt.[7]

In this context, *Killing Eve*'s exploration of sexuality unconstrained by identity is a significant innovation. For example, Eve's sexuality is shaped by complex desires for power, excitement, and danger that transcend identity categories organized around the gender of attraction. In turn, Villanelle's desires center on women, but also encompass her love of attention and showing off. In many ways, the women's dynamic mirrors the poststructuralist writings of Michel Foucault, which explored the interplay of power and pleasure, as part of a broader inquiry into the history of sexuality and knowledge. Foucault saw power and pleasure as co-constitutive, describing "the pleasure that comes of exercising a power that questions, monitors, watches, spies, searches out, palpates, brings to light" and "the pleasure that kindles at having to evade this power, flee from it, fool it, or travesty it." Specifically, Foucault found the relationship between an expert and their subject to be rife with power games, as the expert "lets itself be invaded by the pleasure it is pursuing," while the subject asserts their power "in the pleasure of showing off, scandalizing, or resisting."[8]

Certainly, Foucault's theoretical inquiries and *Killing Eve*'s televised entertainment are radically different projects. Nonetheless, the series' portrayal of sexuality as enmeshed in power dynamics—often combative, frequently pleasurable, and always in flux—bears greater resemblance to the insights of queer theorists than to the conventions of the "lesbian normal" typically found on television.

Queer Craft

Building on its rich depictions of sexual desire, *Killing Eve* also develops inventive methods for bringing queerness into view. First, the series hijacks thriller locations to stage Eve and Villanelle's attractions, redeploying genre settings in erotically charged ways. Early in season 1, for instance, Eve describes Villanelle's appearance to the police:

> EVE: Her hair is dark blonde, maybe honey. It was tied back. Uh, she was slim, about twenty-five, twenty-six. She had very delicate features. Her eyes are sort of catlike. Wide, but alert. Her lips are full, she has a long neck, high cheekbones. Skin is smooth and bright. She had a lost look in her eye that was both direct and also chilling. She's totally focused . . . yet almost entirely inaccessible.
>
> MAN: Uh . . . So, is that like a square face or an oval face?

Spoken in a dreamy tone, Eve's description is funny and surprising, offering viewers a first glimpse of her attraction to Villanelle ("Don't

Eve finds the note that Villanelle included when returning Eve's stolen suitcase ("I Have a Thing About Bathrooms," 1.5).

I Know You?," 1.3). The dialogue draws from John Steinbeck's 1952 novel, *East of Eden*, where the narrator describes Cathy Ames in similar terms, but its setting is even more noteworthy, as *Killing Eve* repurposes procedural convention to spotlight queer desire.[9]

Genre-typical scenes of suspense are likewise transformed. For example, suspicious packages are a thriller cliché, typically sent from killer to cop and containing a sign of imminent violence, such as a threatening note or dismembered body part. *Killing Eve*'s package is far more unusual, as Villanelle returns Eve's stolen suitcase, packed with designer clothing, a bottle of La Villanelle perfume, and a handwritten note that says, "sorry baby, x." Sent in the wake of Bill's murder, the items carry a cruel taunt, but Eve is nonetheless drawn in. As a slow and menacing Unloved track plays, complete with ticking time-bomb sound, Eve breathes in the perfume, then dons a stunning black-and-white Roland Mouret dress. Turning to face herself in the mirror, Eve is confronted with her own erotic potential, as well as the terrifying yet tantalizing knowledge of how she exists in Villanelle's mind ("I Have a Thing About Bathrooms," 1.5).

Villanelle pins Eve to the fridge with a knife while smelling her perfume ("I Have a Thing About Bathrooms," 1.5).

Moments later, the scene morphs into another genre standard—the home invasion—when Villanelle breaks into Eve's house. In true thriller fashion, Eve runs up a narrow staircase and locks herself in the bathroom, only for Villanelle to kick down the door and physically pin Eve in the bathtub. Far less typically, Eve is wearing Villanelle's dress, and Villanelle wants to ask Eve to dinner. *Killing Eve*'s juxtapositions of humor, terror, violence and domesticity drive the scene forward, as the women move to Eve's kitchen and eat leftover shepherd's pie. The tension escalates when Eve suddenly grabs a knife, Villanelle parries, and the two end up flush together, against the fridge, with Villanelle holding the knife to Eve's chest, threatening to "push it in slowly," while marveling that Eve wears her perfume.

Killing Eve even appropriates acts of violence for queer purposes, particularly those involving knives. For instance, when Eve stabs Villanelle in season 1's finale, the entire scene is erotically coded. Not only are the women in bed, having confessed obsessive longings and masturbatory fantasies, but the stabbing itself plays out like a sexual encounter: Eve straddles Villanelle's stomach, stunned by her act of penetration; Villanelle screams, "I really liked you," evoking a jilted lover's heartache; and Eve immediately changes her mind, belying her murderous intent ("God, I'm Tired," 1.8). In a post-screening interview, Waller-Bridge encouraged this interpretation, describing the scene as "a tricky second date" and likening Eve's panic to post-sex regret: "The moment after someone sleeps with someone they know they shouldn't have . . . after they've actually put it in and taken it out again, so to speak, there's the sobering moment of 'Oh God what have I done!?'"[10] Similarly, Woodward Gentle described the scene to me as "pure sex."

Such bold reworkings of thriller conventions enable women's queer desires to surface in unlikely settings. These stretch beyond the everyday spaces that accommodate the "lesbian normal" (such as the school or family), as well as beyond the community and institutional spaces where marginalized characters are often contained (such as the bar or the prison). By occupying and repurposing the standard locations of the thriller, *Killing Eve* expands not only the forms of desire portrayed on television, but also the sites in which those desires can be staged.

Alongside these genre subversions, *Killing Eve* also employs formal audiovisual techniques to bring complex queer desires into view. Most notably, *Killing Eve* uses song lyrics to layer sexual and romantic meanings onto scenes that visually signify threat. In an interview with the BBC, Unloved's vocalist Jade Vincent described her role as that of "a subliminal narrator," who gives voice to Villanelle's "first love with Eve."[11]

For example, when Eve kisses Villanelle on a bus, disarming her in the midst of a fight, Unloved's version of "Strange Effect" shapes its meaning, as Vincent sings: "You've got this strange effect on me / And I like it / You make my world seem right / You make my darkness bright" ("Meetings Have Biscuits," 3.3).[12] Sourced music does similar work. When Eve cuts herself on the lipstick blade, as described above, her facial expressions of intrigue and arousal are amplified by the raucous sounds of "Screw You," by Ramases and Selket, a 1970s psychedelic song that gleefully pronounces twisted desires: "I'm gonna screw you / I'm gonna put a thought right through you" ("The Hungry Caterpillar," 2.3). Displacing dialogue or internal monologue, the lyrics capture the slippery nature of Eve and Villanelle's relationship: the double meaning of "screw," the danger of a penetrating thought, and the uncertainty over who will screw who.

Killing Eve also uses editing to communicate the women's inner lives. In season 2, for instance, a carefully constructed sequence intercuts between two scenes in which both women are deep in thought ("Desperate Times," 2.4). In one, Eve stares into the two-way mirror of an MI6 interrogation room, preparing to question a new assassin. In the other, Villanelle sobs in a hotel mirror, devastated that Eve hasn't arrived to investigate one of her kills. Mirrors recur throughout the series to convey themes of self-reflection, fragmentation, and seeing oneself through another's eyes. In this instance, the parallel staging also signals the women's seemingly fated connection, while the editing conveys their constant entanglement, without the need for dialogue. The soundtrack further enhances these effects, through the single song that unites both scenes: a Dutch-language cover of "Angel of the Morning," which lends the moment an unmistakable emotional charge, but routed through an uncommon language that keeps legibility slightly at bay (Willeke Alberti, "Vlinder Van Een Zomer").

Finally, *Killing Eve* often repeats audio and visual motifs to link otherwise disparate scenes. For instance, when Villanelle murders Bill in season 1, an Unloved track, "Bill," accompanies her actions, with the lyrics: "Don't take him / He's no good" ("Don't I Know You?," 1.3). The song returns in season 4 with altered lyrics, as Eve helps Villanelle after an injury: "Don't take her / She's no good" ("Oh Goodie, I'm the Winner," 4.6). This repetition with a twist signals key shifts in Eve's character and her deepening feelings for Villanelle, even as Villanelle grows impatient with Eve's refusal to put them into words.

Killing Eve also repeats visual cues across seasons, as I will discuss in chapter 4.

Killing Eve's formal innovations offer new ways to render queer desire on-screen. Critically, these audiovisual techniques allow desire to remain unsayable at times. This doesn't signal a return to the shame of the closet, but an embrace of complex desire that exceeds the language required to describe it. Eve wants the woman who murdered her friend. Villanelle wants the woman who hunted and stabbed her. By moving away from dialogue-driven exposition, *Killing Eve* delinks desire from language and reason, creating new space to explore its raw, affective, unprocessed forms.

Queerbaiting

Killing Eve's unconventional approach to representing sexuality sometimes led to accusations of queerbaiting, a media marketing strategy that entices queer audiences with hints of same-gender relationships that ultimately do not materialize. The term was coined in the 2010s to call out television shows that cynically teased same-gender attraction between characters who remained resolutely straight, such as *Supernatural* (The WB/The CW, 2005–20), *Sherlock* (BBC One, 2010–17), and *Rizzoli & Isles* (TNT, 2010–16).[13] The queerbaiting charges against *Killing Eve* reached a peak at the end of season 2, triggered by the season finale and a subsequent interview with Sandra Oh. The controversy points to divergent views about queer representation and the complexities of innovative television.

Queerbaiting accusations are typically triggered by advertising that promises queer visibility. *Killing Eve* certainly made such promises, through marketing that consistently emphasized Eve and Villanelle's erotic charge. The key art for season 1, for instance, featured a close-up of their faces, set against a black-and-red background, with Villanelle's forearm around Eve's throat: intimate, threatening, and deeply seductive. Season 2 art similarly featured the women in close proximity, as Eve held Villanelle around the waist, against a blue

Key art for *Killing Eve* emphasizes the women's erotically charged relationship, as posters for seasons 1 and 2 illustrate.

background streaked with blood, evoking both a crime scene capture and a perverse romantic dance, with Villanelle leaning backward, forcing Eve to bear her weight.

Marketing for season 2 was particularly inventive, utilizing public spaces to stage the women's cat-and-mouse chase. For example, billboards appeared across the UK containing handwritten messages from Villanelle, such as "Have you seen my girlfriend?" and "I thought you were special," while a second round included Eve's scrawled reply: "Okay Villanelle, you've got my attention. Let's talk. 07788 387000." The marketing campaign also included Villanelle hacking BBC One's Twitter account to demand Eve's attention, a phone call to Radio One's breakfast program to request a song for Eve ("Bad Blood" by Taylor Swift and Kendrick Lamar), and playlists the characters "made" for each other, distributed via BBC's *Obsessed With . . . "Killing Eve"* podcast.

Advertising for season 2 promised a queer, obsessive dynamic, and the season delivered in full, offering the series' most erotic and kinky scenes. For some fans and critics, however, these scenes failed to meet expectations of how same-gender desire should manifest on-screen. Most immediately, frustration focused on the finale, which teased a future between the women, after Villanelle slit a man's throat, Eve reciprocated with an axe, and the pair made plans to escape to Alaska where they could be "normal" together ("You're Mine," 2.8). The fantasy crashed quickly, however, when Eve saw through Villanelle's manipulations and walked away, only for Villanelle to gun her down. While many queer viewers loved the episode's bait-and-switch structure, others saw queerbaiting only, claiming that *Killing Eve*'s promise of queer representation had been unfulfilled.

These accusations gained traction when *Gay Times* published a post-finale interview with Sandra Oh and Jodie Comer, reporting that Oh had been "quick to dismiss" a possible romance between the characters. In the interview, Oh explained that such a relationship was not a "focus or a message" of the show, adding, "You guys are tricky because you want to make it into something . . . but it just isn't."[14] Stripped of context, Oh's comments went viral, as fans and critics accused the show of gaslighting viewers by disavowing on-screen queer content and teasing a future that would not come.

The *Gay Times* controversy was, at least partially, manufactured, with Oh's remarks taken out of context. For example, the article omitted the interviewer's question, which obscured the "message" that *Killing Eve* chose not to make. Moreover, elsewhere in the interview, Oh emphasized *Killing Eve*'s focus on complex and expansive desires, stating that "sexuality and discovery of the wider reaches of sexuality is the theme of the show." A similar pattern emerged in an interview with *E! Insider*, where Oh refused to label the relationship "romantic" or "sexual," instead describing it as "a fraught and complex and unconscious drive. . . . I don't want to narrow their relationship into any kind of box."[15] While I might question Oh's definition of the "sexual" as excluding fraught and unconscious desires, her framing aligned with the series' consistent messaging: *Killing Eve* explored same-gender desires beyond the trappings of normative romance and typical identity-based concerns.

The broader context helped to clarify Oh's comments and alleviated many fans' queerbaiting worries. For others, however, references to fluid or nuanced sexuality were insufficient, merely masking television's reluctance to tell queer stories in less evasive ways. These competing interpretations serve to remind us that queer audiences are heterogeneous, with varying media tastes and perspectives on representation. They also point to an intriguing aspect of queerbaiting discourse. If television shows ought to deliver the queerness they promise, what qualifies as proof?

Within *Killing Eve*, a verbal coming out statement was out of the question, since the show set aside sexual identity to focus on the complexities of desire. Verbal expressions of feelings and fantasies could and did happen, but, given the characters' manipulative histories, words perhaps could not be trusted. We might imagine that sex or sex-adjacent actions would confirm same-gender desires, but even this was complicated. After all, season 2 was packed with such actions. These extended beyond the subtext of stolen touches, yearning glances, and double entendres to also encompass direct expressions of shared attraction. In such scenes, Eve got aroused at Villanelle's attentions, Villanelle had sex while thinking of Eve, and Eve listened to Villanelle masturbate, as Villanelle urged Eve to let herself go. Nonetheless, *Vice* magazine lamented the "lack of on-screen steam," and *Variety* protested the endless teasing of queer desire "without a tangible point in sight."[16] These comments do more than point to viewers' different media interests. They also point to the subjective nature of erotics: What is "steam"? What is "tangible"? And who gets to decide?

Instead of trying to answer these questions, *Killing Eve* wrote the conundrum into the script. Specifically, in season 2, Eve visited a psychiatrist to consult about Villanelle's psychopathy, but the conversation quickly shifted to Eve's own psychological state ("Wide Awake," 2.7). When the psychiatrist asked Eve if she and Villanelle were in a relationship, Eve replied: "Define relationship." Her provocation cut to the heart of the show. Define relationship. Define romance. Define queerness. Define sex. By raising those questions, without clear answers, *Killing Eve* did not engage in queerbaiting, but propelled a new and distinctive approach to queer women's television.

3
STUPID WORD

Reimagining Psychopathy

When I asked Waller-Bridge how she would like *Killing Eve* to be remembered, she answered, "Surprising, glorious, and confusingly romantic." These words aptly capture the series' distinctive style and audacious tone, as well as its groundbreaking representations of queer desire. Even more, they speak to the show's central relationship between two psychopath-coded characters: one who yearns for an intimacy that exceeds the terms of her diagnosis, the other who strives to claim parts of herself long held in check. *Killing Eve* may not have set out to expand the ways that psychopaths are imagined onscreen, but, in the process of queering the thriller, it did exactly that.

In this chapter, I focus on the psychopaths of *Killing Eve*. I begin by outlining why this matters, briefly reviewing psychopathy as a psychiatric and cultural category. I then explore specific ways that *Killing Eve* breaks new ground. First, I discuss the series' construction of an amoral cultural universe that blurs the boundary between the normal and psychopathic. Next, I consider diagnostic scenes that challenge psychiatric expertise. Finally, I analyze ways that Eve and Villanelle's character arcs destabilize dominant cultural meanings, by emphasizing the contingencies of diagnosis and claiming a broader emotional range than such characters are usually allowed.[1]

Psychopaths, Psychiatry, and Television

The term "psychopath" appears frequently on television, typically as a metaphor for evil. Its roots, however, are within psychiatry, where it is a highly contested term. General psychology in the US abandoned the category in 1980, instituting the alternative diagnosis of antisocial personality disorder. The term, however, is still used by UK psychiatrists, as well as within the US legal system, primarily as a risk assessment tool. Diagnostic criteria vary across time and place, but usually encompass low empathy, grandiosity, superficial charm, short-term relationships, shallow emotions, proneness to boredom, and persistent violation of legal and social norms. Psychiatrists who use the term typically view psychopathy as a distinct personality disorder that cannot be treated or changed. Consequently, the diagnosis is laden with stigma, predictions of danger, and pessimism, making psychopaths one of psychiatry's most reviled groups.[2]

As scholars within disability studies and mad studies argue, however, diagnostic categories are not neutral descriptors of an objective underlying truth. Instead, they are social constructs, shaped by cultural and institutional forces and subject to contestation and change. These scholars do not dispute the existence of psychological variation or the lived experience of atypical minds. Instead, they interrogate psychiatric meanings, the complex effects of diagnosis, and the cultural life of psychiatric knowledge, as it circulates within popular culture, including on television.[3]

Numerous scholars and practitioners have questioned the legitimacy of psychopathy as a diagnostic classification, citing its deep entanglement with moral judgment. Prominent forensic psychiatrist John Gunn, for instance, dismisses the concept as little more than a shorthand for "bad," with minimal therapeutic value. Similarly, Jarkko Jalava criticizes the field for engaging in a self-serving "psychopathy project" that seeks ownership of a discredited construct for institutional gain.[4] Anchored in notions of moral failure, definitions of psychopathy have changed dramatically over time, reflecting shifting social norms. During World War I, for instance, conscientious objectors in the UK were diagnosed as psychopaths for deviating from patriotic values, while gay men in the mid-twentieth century were policed as psychopaths in the US.[5] Today, the term typically refers to individuals who lack empathy and engage in violence and manipulation. Some writers and advocates, however, propose an alternative neurodiversity framework that recognizes atypical ways of processing emotional, relational, and moral information, without presuming a singular pathological result.[6]

Television rarely addresses such complexities. In popular culture, the term "psychopath" functions as a synonym for "monster," evoking a figure whose internal world and outward behaviors defy human comprehension. Television has driven this narrative, with twenty-first-century complex TV featuring psychopath monster characters at high rates. Although these characters are primarily created for entertainment, they nonetheless shape public perception, as most of what people "know" about psychopaths comes from what they watch on television. On-screen, psychopaths are almost always an emblem of evil, most typically depicted as sadistic or cannibalistic serial killers, such as Hannibal Lecter (*Hannibal*), Joe Goldberg (*You*), Dexter Morgan (*Dexter*), and Paul Spector (*The Fall*). These figures can be thrilling to watch and often become fan-favorite characters. In contrast, television rarely engages with psychopathy as a psychiatric diagnosis, and certainly not with debates in the field.[7]

Against this backdrop, *Killing Eve*'s psychopath storyline stands out as a bold innovation. Although the series is playful in tone, it takes psychopathy seriously as a real-life psychiatric category, raising questions about diagnosis that are rarely addressed on scripted television. Admittedly, its interventions are inconsistent and sometimes tread predictable ground, particularly at the series' end (see chapter 4).

Nonetheless, across multiple scenes and seasons, *Killing Eve* reimagines psychopath characters beyond television's monster formations, expanding possibilities for representation on-screen.

The Normal and the Psychopathic

Most television crime thrillers take place within realistic settings, where an anomalous psychopath character disrupts the moral status quo. *Killing Eve* takes a radically different approach, creating a cultural universe that is always a little off-kilter and unattached to real world norms. In an interview with *Tripwire* magazine, Waller-Bridge described the series as "a meditation on murder, on loneliness, and the potential for a world without conscience."[8] As a result, amorality infuses the show. This not only breaks from thriller conventions but also refuses a moral foundation against which psychopathy can be defined. Just as *Killing Eve*'s queer innovations rest on its creation of a queer cultural universe (see chapter 2), the series crafts a psychopathic world.

Within this anomalous world, a wide range of characters engage in behaviors that blur the lines between the normal and psychopathic. Carolyn, for example, is one of the series' most distinctive characters. She is emotionally distant, socially awkward, intellectually sharp, and deeply averse to cultural conventions, telling her adult daughter, for instance, that she doesn't "have that gene" that enables parents to fake an interest in their child ("End of Game," 3.6). Carolyn also manipulates others and appears unbothered by violence, as long as it serves her needs. In interviews, actor Fiona Shaw suggested that Carolyn might be autistic, although this is never stated on-screen.[9] At times, her behaviors resemble Villanelle's, complicating boundaries between diagnostic categories, as well as between the normal and not.

Multiple secondary characters similarly trouble these lines. These include Julian, a "Good Samaritan" who quickly becomes controlling and violent when he traps Villanelle in his house ("Nice and Neat,"

2.2) and Phil, a vicar who killed his wife while driving drunk ("Don't Get Eaten," 4.2). Villanelle's former teacher, Anna, provides the most unsettling example, engaging in multiple troubling behaviors that are masked by her respectable exterior ("I Don't Want to be Free," 1.7). Specifically, Anna had sex with Villanelle years before, when she was her teenage student and later lies about it to Eve, insisting that Villanelle's account cannot be trusted. When Anna eventually speaks with Villanelle, as an adult, she acknowledges their sexual history, but continues to shirk responsibility, claiming that Villanelle had seduced her. Certainly, Villanelle's larger-than-life gratuitous violence overshadows Anna's actions: As a teenager, she castrated and killed Anna's husband, resulting in the prison sentence that led her to work for the Twelve. Nonetheless, the juxtaposition of the two women raises complex questions about Anna's behaviors, as well as her role in Villanelle's. The point is not that Anna is clearly a psychopath—or that Villanelle, perhaps, is not—but that the process of noting, sorting, and classifying actions as normal or pathological is riddled with ambiguities, often existing independently of those actions' harms.

Although Anna insists that she is "a good person," other secondary characters readily acknowledge their struggles with moral action and meaning. In season 2, for instance, Villanelle attends a twelve-step meeting as part of her undercover work for MI6 ("I Hope You Like Missionary!," 2.6). There, she describes her relationship to emotion: "Most of the time, most days, I feel nothing. I don't feel anything. It is so boring. I wake up and I think 'Again? Really? I have to do this again?' And what I really don't understand is how come everybody else isn't screaming with boredom, too." When the meeting's facilitator responds, "I think we can all relate to that," he normalizes the pervasive boredom that is one of psychopathy's signs. Similarly, the following season, Eve confesses to a coworker, Jamie, that she has endangered her husband's life, stabbed someone, and left a colleague to die. Jamie reciprocates with his own transgressions—giving a best friend drugs that killed him and committing assault and battery—before concluding: "Do not think that you are the only self-loathing arsehole in the room" ("Still Got It," 3.4).

Such scenes disrupt the intense "otherness" of television's psychopath monsters, by repositioning psychopath-coded traits as generalized alienation or unlikeable "arsehole" behavior. The latter recurs throughout the show. Eve, for instance, regularly refers to Villanelle as a "little prick" and an "asshole," while Villanelle dismisses season 2's psychopathic villain, Aaron, as a "dick." This emphasis on bad behavior divorced from a singular monstrosity recontextualizes psychopathy, without denying its potential harms.

Diagnostic Scenes

Killing Eve's focus on "asshole" behavior also sidesteps diagnostic meanings, contributing to its broader disruption of psychiatric expertise. Most notably, the show features several psychiatric sessions that subtly criticize professional norms. In one early example, a psychiatrist who works for the Twelve assesses Villanelle. His goal, however, is not to reduce the risk of harm, but to certify her as sufficiently psychopathic to continue her work as a killer-for-hire ("I'll Deal with Him Later," 1.2). Villanelle appears to pass the test, showing no affect as she recounts her recent kills and views graphic photographs that would likely unsettle a "normal" person. Her performance of psychopathic detachment, however, is interrupted when the psychiatrist hands her a drawing of a woman's face, possibly Anna's, or maybe Eve's. The scene performs important work: Villanelle's visibly shaken reaction suggests an interiority that exceeds her psychopath classification, while the overall diagnostic encounter gestures toward psychiatry's attachments to the category, in ways that facilitate harm.

Season 2 continues this work. In one episode, Eve attends an MI6 seminar on psychopaths, facilitated by a criminal psychiatrist ("Smell Ya Later," 2.5). The presentation is cartoonish and weak, riddled with over-the-top clumsy errors and absurd images, as the word

A criminal psychiatrist gives a presentation on psychopaths to Eve's MI6 team ("Smell Ya Later," 2.5).

"psychopaths" flashes on-screen in comic lettering over a photo of a red sports car. Although viewers later learn that the seminar is a covert attempt to assess Eve's psychological state, it also serves as a parody of psychiatric expertise itself.

For example, Eve asks if it is possible to manage a psychopath for a short time. The psychiatrist replies that he doesn't know. When Eve presses, "Aren't you the expert on psychopaths?," he answers: "Yes, I am. So I know. And what I'm saying is we don't know." This admission lays bare the deep uncertainty that surrounds psychopathy as a diagnostic category, highlighting an ambiguity that television typically obscures. Undeterred, the psychiatrist pushes forward with a dramatic metaphor. To understand a psychopath, he says: "Just take it all away. They're like facsimiles. Copycats. You might as well try to understand a wasp or a stapler, you know, hole punch, telephone." The statement is stark and dehumanizing. It is, however, immediately countered by clever editing that cuts to Villanelle lying with her head in the lap of a young hotel worker, instructing him to stroke her hair. When Villanelle asks if he is lonely, the man admits that he is, describing the difficulty of meeting the right person. Visibly sad, Villanelle agrees. Although her actions are far from conventional, they reveal her emotional vulnerability, undercutting the psychiatrist's claim.

Eve also sometimes positions herself as an expert on psychopaths, although whether this stems from her undergraduate degree in criminal psychology or her fannish interest in women killers remains unclear. In season 1, she tells Bill that Villanelle likely "scores high on the psychopathy scale" ("I'll Deal with Him Later," 1.2). She later delivers the same assessment to Villanelle, after she breaks into Eve's home ("I Have a Thing About Bathrooms," 1.5). Sitting at Eve's kitchen table, the women engage in one the series' most iconic exchanges:

> EVE: I know you're a psychopath.
> VILLANELLE: You should never tell a psychopath they're a psychopath. It upsets them.
> EVE: Are you upset?

In response, Villanelle nods theatrically, mocking Eve with a childish pout that parodies the feeling of being upset. Nonetheless, her flippancy is interlaced with tantalizing hints of sincerity, as she adds that psychopath is a "stupid word."

Killing Eve's diagnostic scenes resonate with key insights from disability studies and mad studies.[10] Scholars working within these fields interrogate psychiatric power, distinguishing between the lived experience of mental illness and psychiatry's classifications and interpretations. They also attend to diagnoses' complex and sometimes contradictory effects. On the one hand, diagnosis can open doors to resources, community, and self-understanding. On the other, it can generate stigma, foster pessimism, and coerce or withhold treatment. Television narratives of psychopaths rarely engage with the politics of psychiatry, either sidestepping the institution or reifying its expertise. In contrast, *Killing Eve*'s characters push at the boundaries of its authority, questioning the stability of "psychopath" as a cultural and clinical term.

Eve

Eve and Villanelle's character arcs also diverge from typical psychopath storylines. For example, Eve's emotional and narrative journey reveals the contingencies of diagnosis, by contrasting her troubling behaviors with the absence of psychiatric intervention. Throughout the series, Eve engages in numerous impulsive and violent actions that might warrant diagnosis, beginning in earnest when she stabs Villanelle. Although Eve seems to regret the action, her troubling behaviors intensify. At first, these are worrying but inconsequential: She snatches candy from a child, considers pushing a man onto train tracks, and vandalizes the room of Niko's friend, Gemma, while taunting the woman for being afraid. Soon, however, her actions cause significant harm. She directs Villanelle to torture a suspect, leaves a coworker to bleed to death, kidnaps a child, and gouges out another assassin's eyes. Ultimately, Eve kills three times during the series, axing Villanelle's handler to death, crushing another underfoot, and shooting one of the Twelve's founders, although he is unarmed.

Eve's pursuit of knowledge, excitement, sex, and violence are interwoven throughout the series. The question of what to make of her actions, however, remains unanswered, driving the show's heady thrills. On the one hand, her troubling behaviors bloom under the light of Villanelle's attention, suggesting a familiar corruption arc. On the other, her visceral interest in women killers is on display from the start. In the series' very first episode, Eve sits in her home office, surrounded by books and newspaper clippings about women killers and assassins ("Nice Face," 1.1). Here, she describes a graphic fantasy of killing her husband and refers to a photograph of murder as "cool." More dramatically, she also sticks a knife in her thigh, piercing her

Eve cuts her thigh with a knife in the pilot episode ("Nice Face," 1.1).

skin to draw blood and recreate the fatal draining of a femoral artery in one of Villanelle's recent kills. The scene establishes Eve's off-kilter interest in women assassins, as well as her drive for intimate understanding via her body that hints at sex. It also suggests an immunity to the horror of violence, one of psychopathy's cultural and diagnostic signs.

An earlier version of the scene leaned more heavily into its erotics. In the draft script, Eve sits in her home office, beneath a poster of the fictional assassin Nikita, where she contemplates CCTV footage before beginning to masturbate. Other deleted, suggestive scenes include Bill teasing Eve about her "hot little Nikita fantasy" and framing her interest in women killers as a "wet dream."[11] Waller-Bridge laughed when I asked her about those scenes:

> Ha! I'd forgotten about those. We were right to cut them! They were the more on-the-nose, early draft moments when you point out the subtext so glaringly. One of the best parts of rewriting is culling all the "IN CASE YOU HADN'T NOTICED" beats like this. Masturbating

> at the CCTV—oh man that made me cringe laugh now. That is the clunky version of what became her cutting her own leg, which says much more about the complexity of her intrigue in the whole idea of murder and violence, than her simply getting off sexually on watching an assassination.

The complexity of Eve's intrigue is one of the series' key innovations, creating space for a character whose motivations and compulsions are often more baffling than Villanelle's. By dialing back the pilot episode's overt eroticism, *Killing Eve* cultivates a deliberate ambiguity. The knife in the thigh could be kinky, or psychopathic, or neither, or both. Psychiatry itself would be unsure. After all, kink sexuality is a secondary sign of psychopathy. *Killing Eve*'s refusal to resolve these tensions exposes the instability of diagnostic meaning and the limits of categorization itself.

Although Eve demonstrates a clear fascination with blood and violence, as well as a proven ability to kill, she does not fit the typical mold of television's psychopath monsters. In part, this is a matter of context. Like Villanelle, Eve is easily bored, prone to violence, self-absorbed, and dismissive of other people's needs. Unlike Villanelle, however, she is middle-aged, married to a man, and employed by government security services. In this context, her restlessness can easily be read as typical midlife malaise, while her fixation on violence is partially concealed by the structure of her job.

Additionally, as a Korean American woman in her forties, Eve doesn't fit the white (and typically younger) profile of television's psychopath villains, like Hannibal Lecter, Dexter Morgan, Joe Goldberg, Alice Morgan, and Villanelle. Certainly, Asian women have long been cast as stereotypical "dragon ladies," marked by emotional emptiness, sexual excess, and manipulation.[12] As I discussed in chapter 1, however, *Killing Eve* pays little attention to Eve's Asian American identity, and the racialization of psychopath tropes is unexplored. The series does briefly include a Korean woman assassin, nicknamed The Ghost, who moves undetected through corporate spaces disguised as an immigrant service worker. Although her storyline mostly functions to reunite Eve and Villanelle, the character also points to ways that Asian women are overlooked, paralleling Eve's ability to escape scrutiny, except by Villanelle.

Eve's storyline exposes the gap between psychopathic behaviors and diagnosis, underscoring the contingencies of psychiatric intervention and classification. In doing so, it expands the ways that psychopathy is depicted on television. Certainly, cat-and-mouse thrillers often feature corruption arcs that blur the boundary between the hunter and hunted, as seen in *Hannibal* and *Luther*, for instance. *Killing Eve* is the first, however, to frame this dynamic in explicitly psychiatric terms.

Villanelle

Villanelle's character arc also upends television narratives of fictional psychopaths, primarily (but not exclusively) via her attachments to Eve. At the start of the series, Villanelle appears as a recognizable psychopath. She kills with abandon, within and beyond the bounds of her job. She isn't sadistic, but she does take childish delight in her kills. She also is frequently bored and manipulative, lacking empathy and remorse. As the series progresses, however, Villanelle claims an emotional range that challenges the ways that psychopaths are imagined on-screen.

Initially, *Killing Eve* depicts psychopathy as a metaphor for freedom, in clear alignment with previous shows. For example, media scholar Adam Kotsko has analyzed the popularity of television's fictional psychopaths, arguing that they allow viewers to fantasize about life beyond moral or social constraints.[13] Kotsko focuses on the sociopathic heterosexual men of early quality television, such as Don Draper (*Mad Men*, AMC, 2007–15) and Tony Soprano (*The Sopranos*). His insights, however, are even more relevant to the queer women of *Killing Eve*, who pursue psychopathic pleasures and dangers typically reserved for men. Waller-Bridge explained to me how she imagined Villanelle as a psychopath:

> One of the joys of writing Villanelle, was writing a woman without fear. I think women particularly suffer from an unexplained guilt complex, even when we do things that are reasonable like needing to rest on the days when we have heavy period pains. Eve exists entirely in that space. She has compartmentalized herself into someone quiet and apologetic and has sat on any wild spark of her own. Villanelle was free of that shame; yes, she murdered—which isn't ideal—but metaphorically she lived outside of the rules without apology and there is something thrilling and inspiring about a woman doing that.

Treating psychopaths as symbols of freedom can do powerful cultural work, especially when that psychopath is Villanelle, a queer woman who disrupts heteronormative conventions with flamboyant violence and euphoric glee. At the same time, treating psychopaths as *only* a metaphor—whether for freedom or for evil—risks flattening characters' complex personhood in ways that reinscribe psychiatric control.

Killing Eve largely avoids this trap by granting Villanelle a more expansive personality than fictional psychopaths are typically allowed. In part, this comes from her sense of humor, as I discussed in chapter 1. It also emerges from her palpable interest in greater connection and belonging, even before her entanglement with Eve. As her relationship with Eve develops, however, these desires intensify and the interplay of psychopathy and emotionality become one of the series' central concerns.

In early seasons, Villanelle's interest in intimate connection bubbles up unexpectedly, as when she wants to watch a movie or cook for Eve. Just as quickly, those moments collapse under the weight of recurring violence. In contrast, season 3 grants Villanelle more space for self-reflection and emotional growth. Written by Suzanne Heathcote, the season received mixed reactions, with many viewers criticizing its "softer" portrayal of Villanelle.[14] Certainly, the characterization evokes familiar media narratives that explain and contain women's violence with reference to a tragic past (see chapter 1). At the same time, it allows the series to treat psychopathy as more than a metaphor for freedom and to grapple with the complexities of living with a pathologized, nonnormative mind.

During season 3, for example, Villanelle speaks back against popular narratives of psychopathy that others have used to explain her behavior. Most strikingly, during a disastrous visit to Russia, she confronts her mother about the abuse she received as a child, including her mother's decision to abandon her at an orphanage. Unsurprisingly, the scene ends in spectacular violence, as Villanelle kills her mother and burns down the family house, but not before she identifies the claim that she was "bad from the beginning" as a "bullshit myth" that her mother perpetuated to absolve herself of blame ("Are You from Pinner?," 3.5).

Villanelle's changing emotional state leads her to contemplate life beyond killing. It also leads to a new dynamic with Eve. In season 3's finale, for instance, the pair meet at a London ballroom, where they share a touchingly awkward and tender dance. As elderly couples circle around them, a newly vulnerable Villanelle remarks: "It's nice to watch them. They seem happy, carefree . . . I want to feel like that" ("Are You Leading or Am I?," 3.8).

The question of whether Villanelle *can* feel like that follows the women to Tower Bridge for season 3's final scene, where they engage in a conversation that directly challenges television's conflation of psychopathy with monstrosity:

VILLANELLE: Did I ruin your life? Do you think I'm a monster?
EVE: You're so many things.
VILLANELLE: Doesn't answer my question.

EVE: I think we all have monsters inside of us. It's just that most people manage to keep theirs hidden.
VILLANELLE: Well, I haven't.
EVE: No. Neither have I.
VILLANELLE: I think my monster encourages your monster. Right?
EVE: I think I wanted it to.

The scene acknowledges the allure of television's psychopath monsters (Eve "wanted it"), but it also exposes the limits of such representations, as obscuring the "many things" that make up a person. Notably, Eve does not deny Villanelle's badness. Instead, she normalizes it through generalization, while also taking responsibility for monstrous urges of her own ("Are You Leading or Am I?," 3.8).

The scene's staging is also important. Reproducing the theatrics of a classic Western gunman's duel, the women stand back-to-back and then pace away from each other—a visual cue for incoming gunfire that makes its absence all the more clear. The moment also recalls season 2's finale, when Villanelle shot Eve for walking away. The Tower

Eve and Villanelle stand back-to-back on Tower Bridge before walking away from each other in season 3's final scene ("Are You Leading or Am I?," 3.8)

Bridge scene is heavily romance-coded, accompanied by an aching love song with the lyrics "Tell me I'm your baby, and you'll never leave me" (Johnny Jewel featuring Saoirse Ronan, "Tell Me"). It also offers a defiant rebuttal to psychiatric pessimism, asserting the diagnosed psychopath's capacity for self-reflection, curiosity, and change.

On television, psychopath characters usually function as symbolic, monstrous "others," imagined to possess a unique and immutable psychic structure, devoid of emotion, humanity, or depth. Villanelle's desires for Eve complicate these assumptions, troubling diagnostic and cultural limits on what psychopaths are permitted to want or feel. Throughout *Killing Eve*, Villanelle remains a psychopath, but the meaning of that designation stretches and shifts, as she and Eve refuse to let it negate other dimensions of personhood. Together with Eve's character arc, Villanelle's storyline resists the limits of monster narratives, gesturing toward new possibilities beyond the normalcy that psychopathy disrupts and the isolation it typically implies. In doing so, the series carves out critical space—at least temporarily—to reimagine atypical psychologies as sites of connection, recognition, and care.

4
SORRY TO DISAPPOINT

The Pleasures and Pitfalls of Queer Character Death

After four seasons and five years, *Killing Eve* ended on April 10, 2022. Like many other die-hard fans, I watched the finale in real time, checking my social media feed during commercial breaks to share in viewers' collective excitement. The episode teased a hopeful ending, only to pivot in the final minutes, as Villanelle was abruptly killed by a sniper, shortly after kissing Eve and defeating the Twelve. Audience reactions were swift and critical, coalescing into a backlash that centered on the "bury your gays" trope, a widely criticized storytelling convention that kills queer characters as soon as they've served their narrative purpose. Alleging homophobic writing, the backlash cast a long shadow that complicates *Killing Eve*'s reputation as groundbreaking queer television.

In this chapter, I attend to those complications. First, I examine the ending itself, both as it appeared on-screen, and as it was framed in published interviews with *Killing Eve*'s creators. Next, I address the audience backlash, exploring the "bury your gays" allegations and the cultural conditions that helped them converge. Finally, I consider the backlash's reach, including new insights from executive producer,

Sally Woodward Gentle. Throughout, I argue that *Killing Eve*'s ending complicates but does not negate its status as milestone TV.

This chapter omits criticisms that are commonly directed at television shows. For example, allegations of bad writing are frequently leveled at series' finales, such as those of *Game of Thrones* (HBO, 2011–19), *Lost* (ABC, 2004–10), and *Dexter*. Numerous scholars have examined this phenomenon, highlighting industry factors that contribute to the decline of series over time. Here, however, I set aside general critiques to focus instead on the more specific and striking charge: that the groundbreaking queer show, *Killing Eve*, delivered a homophobic end.

Hello, Losers

As I've argued throughout the book, *Killing Eve* subverts the cat-and-mouse thriller for queer ends, centering the strange and strangely compelling relationship of Eve and Villanelle. For most of the series, the unlikely love story takes place at a distance, routed through objects, other people, and violence. The finale ("Hello, Losers," 4.8), however, unites the women for the duration, after Eve tracks Villanelle to a remote Scottish island, gouges out another assassin's eyes, and escapes with Villanelle by her side. The episode is playful and romantic, *Killing Eve* style. The two women taunt each other and mock a couple they meet in a rainstorm. They argue on a country road, only for Villanelle to lift Eve up and spin her around: invasive, childish, intimate, fun. One minute they joke about murder; the next they do the dishes together. They share a sleeping bag, split fries, and drive cross-country in a stolen camper van as Eve tosses candy into Villanelle's mouth, while "Don't You Want Me?" by the Human League plays on the radio, continuing the show's reliance on '80s pop for its rare diegetic tracks. "Hello, Losers" functions as a honeymoon episode and series conclusion, steeped in callbacks to the show's most iconic scenes.

Television finales often feature "curtain calls," which bring back favorite characters for a final goodbye. *Killing Eve*, however, bids those

Season 4's sleeping bag scene is staged to parallel season 1's bed scene, as highlighted in advertising for season 4.

farewells in its penultimate episode, via a karaoke flashback, reserving "Hello, Losers" for memories of Eve and Villanelle. The finale's shared sleeping bag scene, for example, is carefully staged to replicate season 1's shared bed scene, when Eve stabbed Villanelle in Paris. In "Hello, Losers," the scene is reworked: Villanelle touches Eve's gunshot scar in wordless apology, before inviting her to steal a camper van, evoking a twisted marriage proposal, as Eve dreamily answers, "Yes." Similarly, when the women eat fries at a roadside cafe and accuse each other of being psychopaths, it calls up season 1's kitchen scene, when Eve questioned Villanelle about her psychopathy over microwaved shepherd's pie. Finally, when the women share a romantic kiss after urinating together at the side of the road, the scene is layered with multiple callbacks: their first ever meeting in a bathroom and the first hints of romance on a Bletcham country road. Even the music (The Mistys, "Bite Marks"), is ripped from the playlist that Eve "made" for Villanelle, as part of season 2's marketing campaign.

Once the women reach London, the action picks up. They locate the Twelve on a Thames riverboat, Villanelle gasses the boat's kitchen crew, and Eve officiates a wedding between two men, delivering a speech that compares love to the Japanese art of Kintsugi. Looking directly at Villanelle, Eve speaks of the beauty of relationships built of broken parts, referencing their own relationship, but also perhaps the episode structure, which reassembles their troubled history into the promise of something new. Villanelle then slips downstairs and removes her jacket, revealing a slate gray tank top that mirrors Eve's clothing from season 2's iconic kitchen scene. In a split screen, Villanelle kills the Twelve with her bare hands, as Eve dances the electric slide in celebration. Bathed in blue light, the kill scene evokes Villanelle's murder of Bill in a nightclub, but her violence now serves Eve's interests, who reclaims the dance floor as her own.

It is *Killing Eve*'s version of a happy ending—violent and tender—until it isn't. As Eve and Villanelle hug on the deck, a bullet strikes Villanelle in the back, with echoes of the time she shot Eve. Suddenly, the season callbacks take a more ominous turn. Against the backdrop of Tower Bridge, the site of season 3's hopeful finale, an injured Villanelle rushes Eve over the railing, into the river, where the women drift apart. More bullets strike Villanelle and blood blooms from her body as angel wings, beneath a stream of bright white light. In a

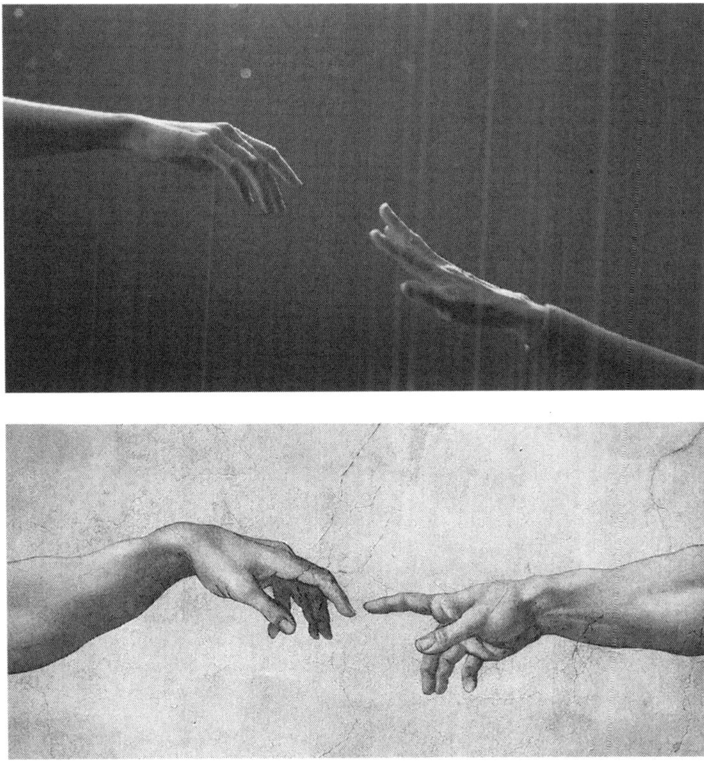

In *Killing Eve*'s final scene, Eve and Villanelle reach for each other in the River Thames, in a replication of Michelangelo's sixteenth-century painting *The Creation of Adam* ("Hello Losers," 4.8).

recreation of Michelangelo's sixteenth-century painting *The Creation of Adam*, Eve reaches for Villanelle's outstretched hand, but fails to connect, as the current drags Villanelle away. Scored with Unloved's somber music (Jade Vincent singing "I die a little"), the scene cuts to Carolyn, speaking into a two-way radio, confirming her order of Villanelle's death. In one last call-out to earlier seasons, Eve emerges from the water, screaming, replicating her series debut, when she had woken in bed, screaming, after falling asleep on her arms. In season 1, Eve's actions had knowingly subverted the thriller genre's "screaming traumatized woman" trope. Now, at the series' end, Eve becomes the traumatized woman, with Villanelle dead in the water beneath her, as *Killing Eve*'s signature title card blazons THE END across the screen.

Killing Eve's ending was stunningly cruel. I personally liked it. I interpreted the final episode and its closing scene as a bold display of queer defiance in the face of inevitable death. For me, this inevitability was not the product of Villanelle's crimes or psychopathy, but her humanness and mortality—unavoidable facts for us all. Life ends. Death happens. It's rarely logical, meaningful, or fair. Much of the time, we don't see it coming. This raises the question: How do we live in the wake of that knowledge? I viewed "Hello, Losers" as offering one answer. Live fully, in the moment: Be with loved ones, eat, laugh, dance, fight, make out on the side of the road. Certainly, it wasn't the ending I'd hoped for, and it didn't subvert genre conventions in the ways I've explored in this book. Nonetheless, I found it meaningful. It was good enough.

My interpretation, however, was out of step with most critics and online fans. Reviewers instantly slammed the show for a rushed and anticlimactic ending that abandoned the promise of *Killing Eve*. *Vanity Fair* described it as "stereotypical and exhausting," *The Guardian* called it an "almost unforgivable betrayal," and *Forbes* succinctly summarized the collective sentiment: "Everyone hates the *Killing Eve* series finale ending."[1] Of course, not everyone hated it, and alternative assessments occasionally surfaced. Nonetheless, these were drowned out by two perspectives that quickly seized the cultural conversation: the official stance of *Killing Eve*'s creators that emphasized the ending's "emotional truth," and widespread criticism by fans and reviewers that focused on the "bury your gays" trope. Unlike my personal interpretation, these frameworks took root in popular culture and shaped understandings of the show.

Rebirths and Celestial Beings

Within twenty-four hours of the finale's screening, online entertainment media published interviews with executive producer Sally Woodward Gentle and season 4 lead writer Laura Neal. The interviews promised behind-the-scenes insights into the ending, while extending hype for the show. Instead, the interviews stunned viewers—myself included—by imposing conventional notions of reality, normalcy, and morality onto a show that had consistently shunned those constraints.

Most strikingly, the interviews framed Villanelle's death as the inevitable outcome of her violent nature and allegiance to killing.[2] Neal, for instance, described Villanelle's "bloody" end as appropriate, because she was "forged in death and destruction. . . . That's her place, that's where she belongs." Moreover, Neal explained that Villanelle was not fully human, but a "celestial" being who needed to die because she was "too big for this world." As Neal stated: "It's almost like that's what she's destined for. She isn't destined to walk among the earth with people like you and I."[3] Certainly, interviews tempered this framing by claiming that Villanelle had saved Eve's life by pushing her off the boat, demonstrating her capacity for good. Nonetheless, the referendum on Villanelle's goodness was startling for a show that had rejected morality as a central, organizing, narrative force.

The reasons given for Eve's survival were equally striking. Most notably, Woodward Gentle and Neal discussed Eve's survival as a "rebirth," as she emerged from the river, stronger and free of Villanelle. Reviving a character description from season 1, Eve was framed as a plucky "everywoman" who wasn't destined for death or punishment but an "amazing" future. According to Neal, Eve and Villanelle were "intrinsically different" types of people: one who sought life and the other death. This, she stated, was indicated by the finale's dance/kill montage: "Eve has rediscovered life in that moment, and she's amongst human beings, people like her, and she's remembering what the normal world has to offer. And then Villanelle is in the place where she feels happiest, which is blood-soaked, steeped in killing."[4] Given these fundamental differences, Neal explained that Eve's scream was not primarily fueled by grief, but by triumph and relief.

Although the death of a leading character was unsurprising in a show that revolved around killing, the meanings assigned to Villanelle's death—and Eve's survival—clashed with the show's groundbreaking work. Taken together, the interviews framed Villanelle's death as the only imaginable outcome and Eve's survival as a triumphant escape. Neal's interviews even reframed the final episode's romantic and domestic scenes as spaces where the characters tested their relationship, only to discover that it could not work. The interviews' persistent emphasis on morality and reality complicates the show's reputation as cutting-edge queer television.

Author interviews raise a difficult question, however. How much weight should they be given? Television studies scholars debate their value when studying a program's cultural significance. In part, this is because television shows (like any text) are polysemic, carrying multiple meanings that cannot be determined in advance. Consequently, the decision to privilege an author's preferred meaning is simply that: a decision that viewers can choose not to make. Author interviews may also be of limited use because of the circumstances of their creation. As Jason Mittell explains, author interviews are a fairly recent industry development that emerged under specific conditions.[5] Before the 2010s, TV writers and producers were relatively anonymous figures who played a minimal role in network marketing campaigns. Today, however, networks utilize author interviews as a promotional tool, giving audiences unprecedented access to writers and their apparent creative intent. The relationship between these interviews and the realities of television production, however, remains deeply unclear.

For one, television shows are not created by a single author who executes their vision without constraint, but by a team of writers, producers, directors, and editors who work under industry arrangements that are hidden from public view. These include network oversight, production schedules, actor interests, and personnel disputes. As Mittell reminds us, television shows are the product of a "much messier, more collaborative, and contingent [process] than the image of an all-powerful creator with a master plan suggests."[6] As a result, author interviews can overstate TV writers' creative freedom, particularly since labor contracts and confidentiality agreements preclude discussion of workplace constraints. Moreover, because these interviews function as a form of advertising, they are typically curated by network executives who authorize content in advance, making it deeply unclear whose message is being conveyed. Consequently, some scholars suggest that we do not engage with author interviews, allowing shows to speak for themselves.

Despite these cautions, author interviews are now a regular part of the media landscape and viewers routinely turn to them to "understand" a show. Television studies scholar Jonathan Gray usefully classifies author interviews as paratext, a type of supplementary communication that surrounds a main creative work. As such, author interviews are comparable to network-produced podcasts, trailers, and other promotional materials. As Gray explains, paratexts are "subservient" to the main work but nonetheless operate as an "organizing and disciplining force" that aims to direct audience expectations and interpretations. The organizing power of author interviews is particularly heightened following a series finale, as viewers turn to creators to find out "what it all meant." Networks use these interviews to increase viewer engagement, but they sometimes backfire, particularly when they attempt to direct interpretation in an unpopular direction. As Gray notes, author interviews communicate the "politics a text has or is allowed to have in popular culture." As such, they can support or disrupt viewers' favorable interpretations, or confirm their worst fears.[7]

Killing Eve's post-finale interviews disrupted my personal enjoyment of the ending, but for many viewers they had a more destructive effect. By emphasizing the need for reality and normality, the interviews shot down the show's enabling fantasy, which had invited viewers to enjoy its escapist and amoral thrills. The interviews also presented as truth the value judgments that Eve and Villanelle had resisted all series: that Villanelle was only good for violence, that powerful women were "too much," that it was best to be normal and nice. The religious metaphors landed badly too, likely referencing season 4's blasphemous scenes (when Villanelle hallucinated drag king Jesus), but now evoking Christian morality as they assigned meanings to Eve's life and Villanelle's death. The triple blow of Christian-inflected morality, normality, and reality hit queer fans particularly hard. While some viewers bracketed the interviews to focus primarily on the show, others understandably did not. For these viewers, the interviews heightened suspicions that *Killing Eve* had betrayed its queer fans. Regardless of whether the interviews reflected the opinions of Laura Neal, the Sid Gentle team, BBC America, or someone else entirely, they cast a shadow over the show that persists today.

Towards the end of this chapter, I return to the post-finale interviews, when I report on my exclusive interview with Woodward Gentle in 2024. To preserve the chronology of events that accompanied *Killing Eve*'s finale, however, I first explore the backlash that happened when "Hello, Losers" aired.

Bury Your Gays

Criticisms of *Killing Eve*'s ending erupted within minutes of the closing credits. On social media, fans denounced the finale on multiple grounds, including rushed plotlines, uninspired writing, and failure to deliver a meaningful death. One specific criticism, however, rose to the surface: the claim that *Killing Eve* had used the widely reviled "bury your gays" trope.

The "bury your gays" allegations quickly spread beyond fan spaces, morphing into a widespread backlash that upended prior interpretations of the show. Queer and entertainment media led the charge with lengthy critiques in *Refinery29*, *DigitalSpy*, *Collider*, *IndieWire*, *Den of Geek*, *Gay Times*, *Out*, and *Them*. Mainstream news platforms then joined the fray, reproducing fans' social media posts, including those calling Neal a "bitch."[8] Even Luke Jennings, author of the *Villanelle* novellas, slammed the ending in the UK press for harming queer viewers, in particular, calling it "a bowing to convention" that punished Eve and Villanelle "for the bloody, erotically impelled chaos they have caused."[9]

During the following weeks, accusations of homophobia extended into new sites. For example, fans raised money for billboards in London that protested *Killing Eve*'s use of the trope, while *Psychology Today* published an article to help fans understand their post-finale feelings as "appropriate and understandable responses to oppression."[10] Across diverse platforms, *Killing Eve* was not only charged with delivering a disappointing ending, but also with betraying its core audience and promise of queer joy.

It was a stunning denouement for a show that had once been celebrated as "must-see" queer TV. The "bury your gays" accusation quickly became an interpretive consensus, presumed to reflect the truth of the show. Alleging anti-LGBTQ+ bias, these claims carried a political charge that made them difficult to dispute. Nonetheless, the relationship between *Killing Eve* and the "bury your gays" allegations was more complex than it first appeared.

As a descriptive term, "bury your gays" refers to a storytelling convention in which a queer character, usually a woman, is unexpectedly and violently killed. Stories that utilize this convention typically dispose of a secondary queer character to further a main heterosexual character's arc. These deaths often occur soon after a first kiss, cutting short a burgeoning queer storyline to redirect to "safer" terrain. Critics argue that the trope exploits and devalues queer characters, communicating their disposability and foreclosing queer futures. It also punishes queer audiences, as relatable characters are prematurely removed from screen. Critics of the "bury your gays" trope point to its frequent use in contemporary television and resonance with a longer history of queer representation in film, when death was a precondition of inclusion.[11]

"Bury your gays" also refers to an audience-generated interpretive framework that emerged in 2016, when online fans adopted the hashtag #buryyourgays to protest a wave of queer women character deaths on TV.[12] The protest focused on the death of Lexa, a supporting character in *The 100* (The CW, 2014–20)—a young adult sci-fi drama—who was killed after sharing a kiss with the lead character, Clarke. Taking advantage of new industry models of viewer engagement, fans organized a billboard campaign to protest the trope, lobbied companies to remove advertising from subsequent seasons, and secured an apology from the show's producer. Eight years later, critics of *Killing Eve*'s finale frequently invoked *The 100* to contextualize Villanelle's death and underscore their frustration that similar writing persisted in 2022.

The "bury your gays" backlash illuminates the dynamic ways that meanings are created, contested, and circulated via television and other mass media. First, it demonstrates the considerable power of queer women viewers to influence popular cultural conversations within the media environment of the early 2020s. Regardless of its accurate fit, the "bury your gays" interpretive framework took hold of the popular imagination and drove a backlash that continues to resonate.

The "bury your gays" allegations also illustrate the complexities of meaning-making within genre-blurring television. As Jason Mittell notes, genre directs viewers' expectations of programs, by offering implicit instructions on how to interpret events on-screen.[13] In contrast, television shows that play with genre can muddle the interpretive frame. This can foster innovation, as I've argued throughout the book, but it also creates confusion at times, for viewers and creators alike. In the case of *Killing Eve*, creators positioned the show within the lineage of spy and crime thrillers. They also subverted the thriller for consistently queer ends. Many viewers watched the show as queer television and placed its ending within their own viewing histories: an alternate lineage of queer women character death on-screen. For these viewers, Villanelle's fate was not comparable to the deaths of popular fictional psychopaths, like Alice Morgan (*Luther*) or Hannibal Lecter (*Hannibal*), but instead to queer women characters: Lexa (*The 100*), Tara (*Buffy the Vampire Slayer*), Poussey (*Orange Is the New Black*), and more.[14]

The "bury your gays" interpretive framework warrants even closer attention because it does not neatly fit *Killing Eve*. Certainly, there are some similarities. Villanelle was a queer woman, killed suddenly and violently, after her first romantic kiss with Eve. Additionally, in post-screening interviews, the show's creators suggested that her death was inevitable, evoking the logic of "bury your gays." On-screen, however, Villanelle wasn't a secondary figure, but one of two main leads, whose queer desires and relationships structured the series from the start. Additionally, Villanelle's death occurred in the show's final minutes and did not rob her of future screen time, either alone or with Eve.

More importantly, the cultural universe of *Killing Eve* muddied the use of "bury your gays" as an interpretative framework that pinpoints queer disposability. After all, flamboyant killings and meaningless death were central to *Killing Eve*'s viewing pleasures, enticing viewers to suspend reality and revel in theatrical violence, stripped of real world meaning or consequence. As Villanelle killed at least once per episode, *Killing Eve* played with the queer villain trope, whose genealogy parallels that of "bury your gays." The show toyed with the latter trope too, casually killing off secondary queer characters to propel Eve and Villanelle's romantic arc. Undoubtedly, Villanelle's death was qualitatively different, but for reasons that exceed the "bury your gays" framework, as I discuss below.

Cruelty was also part of the show's cosmology. As described in previous chapters, season 1 quickly moved from queer confessions of sexual attraction to a near-fatal stabbing, while season 2 closed down declarations of love with a gun. That gunshot would have left Eve for dead, if the network hadn't renewed *Killing Eve* for a third season. Anticipating nonrenewal, Sid Gentle Films even filmed an alternate ending, featuring Villanelle in an all-black cowboy-style mourning outfit, as she read a book, *How to Get Over Your Ex*, while cruising a woman in a bar. The scene ultimately wasn't used, but it captured the series' hallmark approach to death, cruelty, and twisted humor. When "Hello, Losers" swiftly moved from a kiss to a gunshot, it not only evoked the "bury your gays" trope, but the recurring motifs of *Killing Eve*.

Finally, queerness was at the heart of the show, not relegated to subplots, supporting characters, or temporary narrative devices. As discussed in chapter 2, *Killing Eve*'s approach to queerness diverged from typical identity-based concerns, and some viewers disapproved. Nonetheless, Villanelle was a brazen and bold queer main character, and her relationship with Eve drove the show.

None of this means that the circumstances of Villanelle's death indicate quality queer storytelling, nor that fans are wrong to feel betrayed. It does mean that "bury your gays" is not the best lens through which to view the end. This might sound pedantic. After all, for many viewers what matters most is Villanelle's death, not the terms with which it's described. These terms, however, do matter for media analysis that seeks to untangle the knot of meanings surrounding the show. Laden with histories of homophobia, "bury your gays" allegations carry a weight that threaten to smother *Killing Eve*'s queer innovations. The allegations' instant appeal also precludes alternative critiques. Setting aside the "bury your gays" framework does not signal passive acceptance of homophobia or allegiance to the show. Instead, it creates new space to analyze *Killing Eve*'s ending in more fitting terms.

Undoubtedly, *Killing Eve*'s finale was not successful. How, then, might its errors be viewed, if not through the lens of "bury your gays"? C. Lee Harrington's innovative work on TV endings is instructive.[15]

Harrington draws from scholarship on aging, death and dying to develop an *ars moriendi* for television, identifying characteristics that enable a series to "die" (end) well. For example, Harrington states that a television show should die as it lived, without last-minute tonal or thematic shifts that undermine what came before. She also emphasizes the need for planning, to enable the "dying" to actively shape their own end. The latter refers to networks' need to tell creators exactly when their series will finish, to support the planning of meaningful, well-paced story arcs. Such clarity is rare in the industry (at least in the US), where the length of time a show stays on air is largely driven by economic factors, not by producers' creative desires. Certainly, Sid Gentle Films had greater control over *Killing Eve*'s end date than many production companies, initiating wrap-up discussions with BBC America during the making of season 3, even though a mutual agreement wasn't reached until season 4 was in development. Nonetheless, Harrington's claims about tonal shifts and the value of shaping one's own ending remain relevant, suggesting that the problem with Villanelle's death did not stem from death itself, but from the tonal and thematic disruptions it unnecessarily put into play.

Killing Eve did not promise a happy ending. It did, however, promise "glory," a term that consistently appeared in publicity interviews, and that drove the pleasures of watching the show. Eve and Villanelle were angry, brilliant, dynamite women who refused to stick to the paths they were given. They disregarded societal conventions. They were not nice. They wanted more. They indulged their chaotic and violent desires without concern for impact on others. And *Killing Eve* invited viewers to root for them, to want their triumph. Eve and Villanelle were glorious, gleeful, unabashed "monsters" who mobilized a tantalizing fantasy: That stepping away from designated roles to embrace complex taboo desires need not lead to loneliness and isolation. It was an oddly hopeful and empowering message, certainly key to the show's success. In short, *Killing Eve* incited viewers' hunger for glory. And then it took it away.

A glorious ending for Eve and Villanelle need not have been a happy one. While some fans hoped the women would ride off into the sunset together, many were ready for a devastating yet triumphant death that captured the show's defiant spirit. Instead, the ending of "Hello, Losers" stripped the women of their agency, a term that describes people's ability to exert power, even under significant constraint. Certainly, agency within *Killing Eve* took unconventional forms. Eve and Villanelle hurt each other, engaging in acts of mutual destruction, self-destruction, and self-sabotage. Their violence, however, was self-determined. Together, they directed their fates, even when it ended in blood. The finale, in contrast, kept the blood but abandoned their agency, infusing *Killing Eve*'s typical violence with new meaning that countered all that had come before. For the first time, Eve and Villanelle's separation was not caused by their own actions, but by Carolyn, a government agent who simply wanted to regain her job. I suspect it was this display of powerlessness—rather than Villanelle's death itself—that sparked many viewers' sense of betrayal, which was then expressed through the accessible language of "bury your gays."

The Bigger Picture

Multiple factors shaped the backlash against *Killing Eve*'s finale. Most obviously, the ending itself triggered viewers' intense reactions, further fueled by creator interviews and viewers' personal media histories. However, broader industry and cultural conditions also played a crucial role. As media scholars Rob Cover and Cassandra Milne argue in their analysis of fan reactions to queer character death on television, audience backlashes do not emerge fully formed from unpopular endings. Instead, they are cultural products in their own right, produced under specific conditions that extend beyond the death itself.[16] The widespread backlash against *Killing Eve*'s ending thus points to more than dissatisfaction with a high-stakes narrative choice. It also points to production, industry, and cultural dynamics that shaped how viewers' responses cohered and spread.

Production factors laid the groundwork for viewer disappointment with *Killing Eve*'s ending. As I discussed in the book's introduction, each season had a different lead writer, who was encouraged to put her own stamp on show. This created opportunities for multiple women to lead a writers' room, but it also introduced several problems. First, the absence of a single lead writer led to inconsistent vision and tone, as each season blended the show's hallmark ingredients of violence, humor, cruelty, romance, kink, and tenderness in its own way. Most notably, season 3 (the penultimate season) was largely devoid of cruelty, instead exploring the loneliness that emerged in its wake. It also took a radically new approach to "humanizing" Villanelle, establishing her as a troubled young woman desperate to change, possibly with Eve by her side. Season 3's tonal shift alienated some long-time fans, but it also attracted new viewers, eager for a more supportive and normative romance to blossom during season 4. When season 4 pivoted again, the disrupted storyline frustrated many, setting the stage for viewers' anger with the end. The rotating group of lead writers created other problems, too, preventing viewers from developing loyalty to a single trusted creator, which often can soften storytelling blows. These issues arose from a production model that promised to keep the series fresh, but ultimately didn't work.

If production factors set the stage for disappointment, industry factors played a key role in inciting feelings of betrayal. Certainly, Villanelle's death triggered those feelings, but fans of other TV shows with "bad endings"—such as *Lost* and *Game of Thrones*—have expressed comparable sentiments in remarkably similar terms. Even without queer character death, fans have accused creators of unforgivable viewer betrayal, moral transgressions, violations of character integrity, poor writing, and wasted time.[17]

New models of industry-viewer engagement play a role in stoking such feelings. As Cover and Milne argue, these models are more interactive and transactional than those of the past. Networks now engage with viewers to secure their loyalty, and actively cultivate superfans, whose creative labor generates free publicity for the show. Although series' producers and writers do not oversee these interactions, network-driven marketing strategies nonetheless raise fan expectations that "the show" cares about them and will fulfill their requests. These expectations aren't completely unfounded. In the past, producers have developed queer storylines in response to viewers' wishes, as seen with *Glee*, for instance. They also have apologized for controversial queer representations when criticized by fans, as with *The 100* and *Community* (NBC, 2009–15). Fan communities know of these cases, which increases the sense of betrayal when expectations are not met.

To coalesce into a cultural backlash, individual viewers' feelings needed to find collective expression. New models of online fandom provided the spaces for this to occur. As many scholars have shown, social media platforms have fundamentally changed the television viewing experience, as fans engage in live tweeting to create real-time watch parties and large-scale community events. Under these conditions, disappointment with a program can easily morph from an individual feeling to a collective experience, perhaps reframed as community harm. Social media also allows online fans to share resources that promote their interpretations. Following "Hello, Losers," for instance, online fans posted links to the post-finale interviews and educated each other on the history of "bury your gays." Online fandoms also inadvertently create archives of accessible tweets that journalists mine to bolster their stories. Selecting the most provocative tweets, media reports on fan reactions to "Hello, Losers" accelerated the resultant backlash, suggesting a greater degree of consensus than actually existed.

Social media also facilitated the backlash in smaller but more harmful ways. For example, some online fans pressured others to conform to "correct" interpretations, accusing dissenters of homophobia. I experienced this firsthand; I also heard similar reports from viewers who disengaged from online fandom as a result. Others engaged in review-bombing, death threats, and harassment of the show's creators.[18] To be clear, these behaviors likely stemmed from a small group and should not detract from valid criticisms of the show. Additionally, they were not unique to *Killing Eve* fans. Scholars have described similar behaviors in multiple online fandoms, signaling the excesses of some fan spaces, as well as the normalization of harassment within internet culture more broadly. Nonetheless, they had an outsized effect, negatively skewing online ratings and prompting at least some fans with positive views of *Killing Eve*'s ending to withdraw from online discussions.[19]

Finally, broader cultural conditions enabled the backlash, particularly an intensifying anti-LGBTQ+ political climate and COVID isolation and grief. As I discussed in the introduction, many queer fans identified with Villanelle, as her sexuality, neurodiversity, struggles with conformity, and search for belonging resonated in deeply felt ways. As attacks on LGBTQ+ rights escalated in the US and Europe in the early 2020s, via high-profile hate crimes and waves of anti-LGBTQ+ legislation, Villanelle's status as a queer icon intensified, too, signifying the sexual confidence and bold defiance that many viewers aspired to achieve. In this context, her death at the hands of an anonymous sniper with MI6 ties accrued surplus meaning, cutting short even the fantasy of queer triumph in the face of government attacks.

Similarly, the COVID-19 pandemic intensified viewer attachments to the show. Television viewing increased dramatically in 2020, as public health lockdowns and isolation increased people's need for at-home entertainment and escape. COVID lockdowns also led to increases in online fandom participation, which offered both real companionship and parasocial attachments, as well as ways to pass time. COVID conditions hit many people hard, particularly young queer people who were cut off from social supports. Unprecedented levels of death also entered people's lives, with little available public resources for processing trauma and grief.[20]

Even before the COVID pandemic, scholars explained that television can offer viewers a sense of stability and self-understanding, particularly during difficult times. The endings of television series disrupt this "ontological security," even under optimal conditions, by closing down stories that help some viewers make sense of themselves and the world.[21] Far removed from optimal conditions, *Killing Eve*'s ending aired two years into the pandemic, when many people were still in shock or reckoning with multiple losses: loved ones, jobs, health, homes, and future plans. In this context, as many viewers yearned for fun and the oddly comforting brand of escapism that *Killing Eve* offered, the show delivered reality: Villanelle's death and Eve's grief.

Television producers and writers, of course, are not responsible for the cultural conditions under which their shows are received. Nonetheless, these conditions do significantly influence viewer reception. After all, television is not watched in a vacuum, stripped of context, but in relation to viewers' lives. In the case of *Killing Eve*, difficult cultural circumstances joined with earlier production decisions, new models of industry-viewer engagement, and the growing popularity of online fandoms to create a perfect storm of conditions for watching and processing Villanelle's death. These conditions helped to transform individual feelings of disappointment to collective perceptions of betrayal to community-authored political critique. None of these factors "caused" the backlash that followed *Killing Eve*'s ending, but, without them, it may have been smaller, more contested, or may not have occurred at all. This doesn't make the ending "good" or absolve the creators of responsibility. It does remind us that backlashes are not organic or objective measures of a television series' worth. Instead, they are complex, contingent, cultural products shaped by factors internal and external to the show.

Looking Back

After the post-finale interviews, *Killing Eve*'s creators did not speak publicly about the show again. When writing this book, however, I interviewed Woodward Gentle, who spoke on the record about the finale for the first time. Given the post-finale interviews, I was prepared for Woodward Gentle to defend the ending and insist upon the necessity of Villanelle's death to enable Eve's future happiness. Instead, she described the interviews as "ill-prepared responses" that did not capture the spirit of the show. Moreover, she acknowledged that the ending had "failed" and described her regret at the choices they'd made. Since these comments haven't appeared on record before, I quote at length.

First, Woodward Gentle expressed her understanding of fan disappointment: "I think the end is one of the few moments that we fell into quite traditional storytelling. It let down diehard fans. It also let down our own bar that we'd set for ourselves, which was don't fall into those traps. Last minute we fell into the trap." Woodward Gentle further expressed her wish that they had given Eve and Villanelle a happy ending, where they had "gone off into the sunset together." Moreover, she explained what this alternate ending might have looked like, revealing that some fans' hope for a postscript episode hadn't been far-fetched after all:

> We did have a moment when we were going to shoot a postscript. At one point they were going to be in a little place in Alaska together. The fantasy of just seeing them in this little hut in Alaska would've been gorgeous. We went through the idea of one of them receiving a postcard as well, because that had been such a thing in the series, particularly in season 1. We talked about filming it and literally just burying it online for people to find. It only needed to be three and a half minutes. Really, really short. And we didn't film it and we should have filmed it. If we'd done that, I think it would've given the hope that was needed.

Finally, Woodward Gentle described the production team's response to the "bury your gays" backlash:

> We were mortified. We thought we'd done something that was good, that people would understand. We'd employed a queer US television producer to consult with us and she thought it felt quite satisfying. We also had a lot of queer people contributing to the show, and when we watched the last episode together, they said they loved it. But it just blew up. It didn't work. It didn't happen. It was really painful. Such a shame after so much joy. For us and for a lot of other people, it's left a real sadness.

These comments demonstrate the scale and reach of the viewer backlash. They also demonstrate Woodward Gentle's openness to critique, as she acknowledged the validity of viewers' reactions and expressed sadness as a result. Instead of defending the ending, Woodward Gentle reframed and owned it as a mistake: a well-intentioned creative gamble that simply hadn't paid off. Woodward Gentle's candid admissions underscore the reach and intensity of the backlash, which not only tainted viewers' experiences, but the creators' too.

CONCLUSION

In 2018, *Killing Eve* burst onto television screens as a surprisingly fun and audacious show. In 2022, it slipped away shrouded in sadness, felt by viewers and creators alike. Certainly, all involved parties would have preferred a different outcome. But television is more than a vehicle for entertainment; it's also a site for cultural debate. Over its five-year run, *Killing Eve* transformed the television landscape by redeploying thriller conventions for queer and feminist purposes. It also ignited important discussions about queer visibility on television, focusing on the "bury your gays" trope, queerbaiting strategies, and the persistent centering of whiteness on-screen. Some controversies signaled a mismatch between viewer interests and *Killing Eve*'s focus. Others exposed mistakes on the creators' part. These moments of friction highlight *Killing Eve*'s imperfections, but they also attest to its significance as culturally meaningful, milestone TV.

In valuing *Killing Eve* as innovative, imperfect television, I return to the work of queer scholar and cultural critic José Esteban Muñoz. As discussed in the introduction, Muñoz's concept of disidentification emerges from the creative practices of sexually and racially marginalized groups. It also offers a valuable framework for engaging with uneven media, moving beyond complete acceptance or rejection to consider the ways that texts can be used. In practice, disidentification takes varying forms but it encourages people to grapple with the mixed meanings of popular culture, actively taking, critiquing, and remaking the cultural resources they need.

Despite its controversial ending, there is plenty to take from *Killing Eve*. As I've argued throughout this book, the show transformed the television landscape by subverting the cat-and-mouse thriller to center the complexity and queerness of women's desires. Its iconic characters were chaotic, selfish, and self-determined, brimming with an unabashed queerness and hunger for more—more excitement, more meaning—that was stunning to see on mainstream television. The sexual tension between Eve and Villanelle upended television conventions, too, not only through its electric depictions of queer desire, but also through its emphasis on same-gender erotics delinked from identity, and kink dynamics that flouted popular cultural norms. The show's appropriation of thriller conventions also supported fresh critiques of psychiatric power, which facilitated a reimagining of psychopath characters and hinted at new modes of connection, routed through escapist queer thrills. Although the finale did not fully realize the series' potential, this does not erase the innovations that came before.

For a show that centered the interracial, age-stratified, queer relationship between two bloody (and) brilliant women, *Killing Eve* achieved remarkable cultural reach. Top artists like Olivia Rodrigo and Billie Eilish have referenced the show in their music videos, with Eilish recreating the "Hello, Losers" final scene in a promotional video for her 2024 album, *Hit Me Hard and Soft*. Villanelle's iconic costumes have also been featured in several museum exhibitions, including "Beyond the Little Black Dress" at the National Museum of Scotland, which showcased her season 2 Alexander McQueen gown. The series has also left its mark on queer community spaces and businesses, with numerous restaurants and wedding events companies taking the name Villanelle.

Killing Eve had an even greater impact on the television landscape. The show spawned numerous imitators, such as Germany's *Kleo*

(Netflix, 2022–present) and South Korea's *Inspector Koo* (JTBC, 2021). Creators of the US teen vampire show *First Kill* (Netflix, 2022), the British dark comedy *Sweetpea* (Sky Atlantic/Starz, 2024–present), and the British historical drama *Dope Girls* (BBC One, 2025) have also acknowledged their debt to the show. *Killing Eve* established the viability of middle-aged, violent, queer women characters, paving the way for subsequent series, including *Yellowjackets* (Showtime, 2021–present) and *Dead Ringers* (Amazon Prime Video, 2023). Its queer subversion of masculine genres further reverberated in the spy thriller *Black Doves* (Netflix, 2024–present) and the epic fantasy *House of the Dragon* (HBO, 2022–present). Even the Marvel Cinematic Universe has followed in its footsteps. In the television series *Agatha All Along* (Disney+, 2024), Marvel's first on-screen queer kiss took place between two women: Agatha Harkness, the middle-aged protagonist, and Rio Vidal (Lady Death), whose mannerisms, dialogue, and penchant for knife play were clearly inspired by Villanelle.

Killing Eve was not perfect, and later seasons, in particular, sometimes failed to hit the mark. Nonetheless, a television show need not achieve narrative or political perfection to matter deeply in media history and popular culture. *Killing Eve*'s appropriations of thriller conventions transformed the television landscape, claiming new space for women's complex, queer desires. The cultural afterlife of the series testifies to its durable influence and secures its place in media history as groundbreaking, milestone TV.

NOTES

Introduction

1 I interviewed Woodward Gentle in person at the Sid Gentle Films office in August 2024. I recorded and transcribed the interview and confirmed the accuracy of all quoted material. I interviewed Waller-Bridge via email in January 2025. I integrated her written answers and kept her formatting intact, with light editing for stylistic consistency.

2 Hall, "Encoding and Decoding."

3 Havas, *Woman Up*.

4 Muñoz, *Disidentifications*.

5 See, for example, Eugene Lee Yang's recreation of iconic scenes from *Killing Eve*, dressed in drag as Eve Polastri (Sweeting, "Try Guys' Eugene Lee Yang").

6 Jennings later republished the novellas as one book, *Codename Villanelle*, and authored two sequels: *Killing Eve: No Tomorrow* and *Killing Eve: Die for Me*.

7 Bullard, "How Netflix Changed the World of Book Adaptation."

8 White, "*Killing Eve* EP Sally Woodward Gentle."

9 Stanley, "BBC America Turn Male-Oriented Genre on Its Head."

10 Across four seasons, *Killing Eve* won 50 awards and received 169 nominations.

11 Hale, "30 Best International TV Shows of the Decade"; Abbot et al., "100 Best TV Shows of the 21st Century."

12 Chapter titles are based on quotes from *Killing Eve* episodes, mirroring the show's episode naming conventions.

Chapter 1

1 Mittell, *Complex TV*.

2 *Killing Eve*'s writers and producers consistently used this term in publicity interviews throughout the series.

3 Butler, "Visual Style."

4 Karpovich, "*The Avengers*"; White, *Violent Femmes*.

5 Seed, "Crime and the Spy Genre."

6 Havas, Mártonfi, and Gergely, "Beasts from the East"; Sulimma, "The Plane, the City, the Chase."

7 Broad, "*Game of Thrones*."

8 White, *Violent Femmes*.

9 Yotka, "*Killing Eve*," Igoe, "*Killing Eve* Season 3."

10 Champagne, "Costume Designer Phoebe de Gaye."

11 Dolce Vita, "Switchy Queer Style of *Killing Eve*"; Gutowitz, "*Killing Eve*'s Villanelle."

12 For interviews with the series' costume designers, see Halliwell, "How *Killing Eve* Turns Clothes into Characters"; and Alexander, "*Killing Eve* Season Two." For academic analysis of Villanelle's costumes, see Gilligan and Collins, "Fashion-Forward Killer."

13 For a discussion of the dragon lady trope, see Shimizu, *Hypersexuality of Race*. For discussion of white femme fatale assassins, see White, *Violent Femmes*.

14 For analysis of gender in *Killing Eve*, see Black, "Pleasure, Power and Pathology"; Grübler, "*Basic Instinct* with a Twist"; and Miller, Atherton, and Hetherington, "Agents of Chaos."

15 *The Killing* is a US adaptation of Denmark's *Forbrydelsen*; *The Bridge* is the English-language title for the Danish and Swedish *Bron/Broen*; and *Criminal Minds* is a US police procedural that has inspired multiple spin-offs.

16 Sandberg, "*Killing Eve* Writer Dissects the Scene"; Lindsay, "In *Killing Eve*, Women Finally Aren't the Victims"; Sweet, "Undiluted, Unpatronizing, and Made by Women."

17 Birnbaum, "Sandra Oh on *Killing Eve*"; Fujiwara, "Intersectional Feminist Pleasure"; Feikusová, "Perils of Representation."

18 Eve and Yusuf's relationship was the sole exception.

19 Warner, "Racial Logic of *Grey's Anatomy*."
20 Warner.
21 Outstanding Screenplays, "20 Screenwriting Tips from Phoebe Waller-Bridge."

Chapter 2

1 Datum and Voela, "*Killing Eve*"; Moore, "Piqued."
2 For further discussion of the twentieth century rise of LGBTQ+ visibility in popular media, see Gross, *Up from Invisibility*; and Walters, *All the Rage*.
3 McNicholas Smith, *Lesbians on Television*; Walters, *Tolerance Trap*.
4 Brassington, Ferreday, and Girard, *New Queer Television*. For similar trends toward complexity in television's depictions of sex, see Gibbs, Holzberg, and Lehtonen, *Bad Sex*.
5 For an overview of uses of queer, see Sullivan, *Critical Introduction to Queer Theory*. For foundational work on the queerness of mass culture, see Doty, *Making Things Perfectly Queer*.
6 Sullivan, *Critical Introduction to Queer Theory*; Sedgwick, *Epistemology of the Closet*.
7 Sullivan; Sedgwick.
8 Foucault, *History of Sexuality*, 45.
9 Steinbeck, *East of Eden*, 72. For a description of Steinbeck's influence on Waller-Bridge, see Tamaki, "Phoebe Waller-Bridge Loves Antiheroines."
10 Turchiano, "*Killing Eve* Creator."
11 Glynn, "*Killing Eve*."
12 The song was originally recorded by the Kinks in 1965.
13 Brennan, *Queerbaiting and Fandom*; Ng, "Between Text, Paratext, and Context."
14 Connolly, "*Killing Eve* Interview." Woodward Gentle explained to me that Oh's use of the phrase "you guys" referred to the *Gay Times*' interviewers not the LGBTQ+ community, as some readers assumed.
15 E! Insider, "Sandra Oh."
16 Gutowitz, "*Killing Eve*'s Queer Storyline"; Framke, "*Killing Eve* Season Two Stumbled."

Chapter 3

1 An earlier version of this chapter appeared in the *Canadian Journal of Disability Studies*. See Sears, "Never Tell a Psychopath They're a Psychopath."

2 See Shapland, "Defining the Elephant"; and Jalava, Griffiths, and Maraun, *Myth of the Born Criminal*.

3 See Bruce, *How to Go Mad*; Aho, Ben-Moshe, and Hilton, "Mad Futures"; and Clare, *Brilliant Imperfection*.

4 Gunn, "Psychopathy"; Jalava, "Science of Conscience."

5 Shapland, "Defining the Elephant"; Freedman, "Uncontrolled Desires"; Stein, "Boutilier and the U.S. Supreme Court."

6 Ramirez, "Philosophy of Mental Illness"; Thomas, "I'm a Psychopath."

7 Federman, Holmes, and Jacob, "Deconstructing the Psychopath"; Klin and Lemish, "Mental Disorders Stigma in the Media"; Jalava, Griffiths and Maraun, *Myth of the Born Criminal*.

8 Tripwire Magazine, "Phoebe Waller-Bridge Introduces Us to *Killing Eve*."

9 Ahr, "*Killing Eve*."

10 See Bruce, *How to Go Mad*; Aho, Ben-Moshe, and Hilton, "Mad Futures"; and Clare, *Brilliant Imperfection*.

11 "*Killing Eve* Season 1 Deleted Scenes"; Waller-Bridge, *Killing Eve*.

12 Shimizu, *Hypersexuality of Race*.

13 Kotsko, *Why We Love Sociopaths*.

14 Viewers also criticized a perceived decrease in Eve's screen time and narrative role.

Chapter 4

1 Still, "*Killing Eve* Fans Hated the Finale"; Heritage, "Unrepentant Eff You"; Tassi, "Everyone Hates the *Killing Eve* Series Finale Ending."

2 This discussion is based on interviews published in *Collider*, *TV Line*, *Entertainment Weekly*, *Salon*, *Decider*, and *Elle*. See Lane, "*Killing Eve* Showrunner Laura Neal"; Nemetz, "*Killing Eve* Boss Explains"; Snierson, "*Killing Eve* Producer Breaks Down the Fates"; Stine, "*Killing Eve* Boss"; Zalben, "*Killing Eve* Series Finale"; and Zemler, "How *Killing Eve* Landed."

3 Nemetz; Stine.

4 Zalben, "*Killing Eve* Series Finale."

5 Mittell, *Complex TV*.

6 Mittell, 117.

7 Gray, "Intertexts and Paratexts," 212, 214.

8 Chester, "I Actually Feel Cheated."

9 Jennings, "Villanelle Will Be Back!"

10 Heuchan, "#KilltheTrope"; Estrellado, "Psychological Impact."

11 Cover and Milne, "'Bury Your Gays' Trope."

12 Bridges, "Genealogy of Queerbaiting."

13 Mittell, *Complex TV*.

14 Alice and Hannibal's deaths were depicted more ambiguously than Villanelle's, allowing speculation that they survived.

15 Harrington, "*Ars Moriendi* of US Serial Television."

16 Cover and Milne, "'Bury Your Gays' Trope."

17 Mittell, *Complex TV*, 328–29; Burgess and Jones, "Investigating Consumer Perceptions."

18 These social media accounts were publicly visible in 2022 but have since been deleted.

19 For further discussion of vengeful behaviors in television fandoms, see Cameron, "Toxic Regulation"; and Burgess Jones, "Investigating Consumer Perceptions."

20 For discussion of fandom and COVID, see Kim, Wang, and Kim, "Effects of Online Fan Community." For queer youth and COVID, see Paceley et al., "Beyond a Shared Experience."

21 See Williams, *Everybody Hurts*; and Vaage, "Five Theses."

BIBLIOGRAPHY

Abbot, Kate, Hannah Davies, Gwilym Mumford, Phil Harrison, and Jack Seale. "The 100 Best TV Shows of the 21st Century." *Guardian*, September 16, 2019. https://www.theguardian.com/tv-and-radio/2019/sep/16/100-best-tv-shows-of-the-21st-century.

Aho, Tanja, Liat Ben-Moshe, and Leon J. Hilton. "Mad Futures: Affect/Theory/Violence." *American Quarterly* 69.2 (2017): 291–302.

Ahr, Michael. "*Killing Eve*: Fiona Shaw Is the Third Female Lead." *Den of Geek*, May 29, 2018. https://www.denofgeek.com/tv/killing-eve-fiona-shaw-is-the-third-female-lead/.

Alexander, Ella. "*Killing Eve* Season Two: Six Key Looks Analyzed." *Harper's Bazaar*, June 7, 2019. https://www.harpersbazaar.com/uk/fashion/g27479601/killing-eve-season-two-costumes/.

Birnbaum, Debra. "Sandra Oh on *Killing Eve* and If She'd Ever Return to *Grey's Anatomy*." *Variety*, April 6, 2018. https://variety.com/2018/tv/news/sandra-oh-killing-eve-greys-anatomy-1202746281/.

Black, Audrey Jane. "Pleasure, Power and Pathology—Between Two Worlds: *Killing Eve*'s Queer/Feminist Post–Cold War Appraisal." *Feminist Media Studies* 22.4 (2022): 800–815.

Brassington, Thomas, Debra Ferreday, and Dany Girard, eds. *New Queer Television: From Marginalization to Mainstreamification*. Intellect Books, 2025.

Brennan, Joseph. *Queerbaiting and Fandom: Teasing Fans Through Homoerotic Possibilities*. University of Iowa Press, 2019.

Bridges, Elizabeth. "A Genealogy of Queerbaiting: Legal Codes, Production Codes, 'Bury Your Gays,' and '*The 100* Mess.'" *Journal of Fandom Studies* 6.2 (2018): 115–32.

Broad, Leah. "*Game of Thrones*: Music in Complex TV." *Music and the Moving Image* 13.1 (2020): 21–42.

Bruce, La Marr Jurelle. *How to Go Mad Without Losing Your Mind: Madness and Black Radical Creativity*. Duke University Press, 2021.

Bullard, Harper. "How Netflix Changed the World of Book Adaptation." *Publishing Research Quarterly* 39 (2023): 120–31.

Burgess, Jacqueline, and Christian Martyn Jones. "Investigating Consumer Perceptions of Brand Authenticity in a Narrative Brand Ending." *Journal of Product and Brand Management* 32.8 (2023): 1274–86.

Butler, Jeremy. "Visual Style." In *The Craft of Criticism*, edited by Michael Kackman and Mary Celeste Kearney, 59–71. Routledge, 2018.

Champagne, Christine. "Costume Designer Phoebe de Gaye Brings Killer Style to *Killing Eve*." *The Credits*, May 16, 2018. https://www.motionpictures.org/2018/05/costume-designer-phoebe-de-gaye-brings-killer-style-to-killing-eve/.

Chester, Jason. "I Actually Feel Cheated." *Daily Mail*, April 11, 2022. https://www.dailymail.co.uk/tvshowbiz/article-10707427/Killing-Eve-ends-bang-splash-fans-slam-underwhelming-finale.html.

Clare, Eli. *Brilliant Imperfection: Grappling with Cure*. Duke University Press, 2017.

Connolly, William. "*Killing Eve* Interview: Sandra Oh and Jodie Comer Discuss Their Characters' Sexuality." *Gay Times*, June 4, 2019. https://www.gaytimes.com/originals/killing-eve-season-two-interview/.

Cover, Rob, and Cassandra Milne. "The 'Bury Your Gays' Trope in Contemporary Television: Generational Shifts in Production Responses to Audience Dissent." *Journal of Popular Culture* 56 (2023): 810–23.

Datema, Jessica and Angie Voela. "*Killing Eve*: Inflections of Rebirth and Pathogenesis." In *Movement, Velocity, and Rhythm from a Psychoanalytic Perspective: Variable Speed(s)*, edited by Jessica Datema and Angie Voela, 19–57. Routledge, 2023.

Dolce Vita, Anita. "The Switchy Queer Style of *Killing Eve*'s Villanelle." *DapperQ*, May 29, 2019. https://www.dapperq.com/2019/05/the-switchy-queer-style-of-killing-eves-villanelle/.

Doty, Alexander. *Making Things Perfectly Queer: Interpreting Mass Culture*. University of Minnesota Press, 1993.

E! Insider. "Sandra Oh Says *Killing Eve* Season 2 Is 'Bad in a Bad Way.'" YouTube video, 3:01, April 5, 2019, https://www.youtube.com/watch?v=p9bpLowisN8.

Estrellado, Jan. "The Psychological Impact of the *Killing Eve* Series Finale." *Psychology Today*, June 24, 2022. https://www.psychologytoday.com/us/blog/authenticity-and-social-justice/202206/the-psychological-impact-of-the-killing-eve-series.

Federman, Cary, Dave Holmes, and Jean Daniel Jacob. "Deconstructing the Psychopath: A Critical Discursive Analysis." *Cultural Critique* 72.1 (2009): 36–65.

Feikusová, Klára. "The Perils of Representation: Sandra Oh in *Killing Eve*." *Quarterly Review of Film and Video* 41.8 (2023): 1207–31.

Foucault, Michel. *The History of Sexuality: An Introduction*. Vol. 1. Vintage, 1990.

Framke, Caroline. "*Killing Eve* Season Two Stumbled Where *Barry* Soared." *Variety*, May 26, 2019. https://variety.com/2019/tv/columns/killing-eve-season-2-finale-barry-hbo-1203224853/.

Freedman, Estelle. "'Uncontrolled Desires': The Response to the Sexual Psychopath, 1920–1960." *Journal of American History* 74.1 (1987): 83–106.

Fujiwara, Lynn. "Intersectional Feminist Pleasure and the Bind of Heteronormativity in *Killing Eve*." In *The Routledge Companion to Intersectionalities*, edited by Jennifer C. Nash and Samantha Pinto, 459–70. Routledge, 2023.

Gibbs, Jacqueline, Billy Holzberg, and Aura Lehtonen. *Bad Sex: Sexuality, Gender and Affect in Contemporary TV*. Bloomsbury, 2025.

Gilligan, Sarah and Jacky Collins. "Fashion-Forward Killer: Villanelle, Costuming, and Queer Style in *Killing Eve*." *Film, Fashion, and Consumption* 10.2 (2021): 353–76.

Glynn, Paul. "*Killing Eve*: How the Hit BBC Show's Killer Soundtrack Was Made." *BBC*, October 31, 2018. https://www.bbc.com/news/entertainment-arts-45828680.

Gray, Jonathan. "Intertexts and Paratexts." In *The Craft of Criticism*, edited by Michael Kackman and Mary Celeste Kearney, 207–18. Routledge, 2018.

Gross, Larry. *Up from Invisibility: Lesbians, Gay Men, and the Media in America*. Columbia University Press, 2001.

Grübler, Christina. "*Basic Instinct* with a Twist: How the Femmes Fatales of *Killing Eve* Queer the Gendered Politics of Crime Television.' *Gender Forum* 79 (2021): 36–57.

Gunn, John. "Psychopathy: An Elusive Concept with Moral Overtones." In

Psychopathy: Antisocial, Criminal, and Violent Behavior, edited by Theodore Millon, Erik Simonsen, Morten Birket-Smith and Roger D. Davis, 32–39. Guilford, 1998.

Gutowitz, Jill. "*Killing Eve*'s Queer Storyline Is Looking More and More Like a Marketing Ploy." *Vice*, June 6, 2019. https://www.vice.com/en/article/fans-accuse-killing-eve-sandra-oh-of-queerbaiting-after-season-2-finale/.

Hale, Mike. "The 30 Best International TV Shows of the Decade." *New York Times*, December 20, 2019. https://www.nytimes.com/2019/12/20/arts/television/best-international-tv-shows.html.

Hall, Stuart. "Encoding and Decoding in the Television Discourse." In *Writings on Media: History of the Present*, edited by Charlotte Brunsdon, 247–66. Duke University Press, 2021.

Halliwell, Kate. "How *Killing Eve* Turns Clothes into Characters." *The Ringer*, May 14, 2018. https://www.theringer.com/2018/05/14/tv/killing-eve-clothes-pink-dress-phoebe-de-gaye.

Harrington, C. Lee. "The *Ars Moriendi* of US Serial Television: Towards a Good Televisual Death." *International Journal of Cultural Studies* 16.6 (2012): 579–95.

Havas, Júlia, Anna Mártonfi, and Gábor Gergely. "Beasts from the East: Fantasies of Eastern Europeanness in Brexit-Era BBC Drama." *View: Journal of European Television History and Culture* 10.20 (2021): 48–63.

Havas, Júlia. *Woman Up: Invoking Feminism in Quality Television*. Wayne State University Press, 2022.

Heritage, Stuart. "An Unrepentant Eff You." *Guardian*, April 23, 2022. https://www.theguardian.com/tv-and-radio/2022/apr/23/killing-eve-finale-series-bbc.

Heuchan, Claire. "#KilltheTrope: *Killing Eve* Fans Protest 'Bury Your Gays' Ending." *AfterEllen*, June 24, 2022. https://afterellen.com/killthetrope-killing-eve-fans-protest-bury-your-gays-ending/.

Igoe, Katherine. "*Killing Eve* Season 3: Everything We Know." *Marie Claire*, April 10, 2020. https://www.marieclaire.com/culture/a29426399/killing-eve-season-3/.

Jalava, Jarkko, Stephanie Griffiths, and Michael Maraun. *The Myth of the Born Criminal: Psychopathy, Neurobiology, and the Creation of the Modern Degenerate*. University of Toronto Press, 2015.

Jalava, Jarkko. "Science of Conscience: Metaphysics, Morality, and Rhetoric in Psychopathy Research." PhD diss., Simon Fraser University, 2007.

Jennings, Luke. *Codename Villanelle*. John Murray, 2017.

Jennings, Luke. *Killing Eve: Die for Me*. John Murray, 2020.

Jennings, Luke. *Killing Eve: No Tomorrow*. John Murray, 2018.

Jennings, Luke. "'Villanelle Will Be Back!': *Killing Eve*'s Author Speaks Out over the Catastrophic TV Finale." *Guardian*, April 22, 2022. https://www.theguardian.com/tv-and-radio/2022/apr/22/killing-eve-writer-tv-finale.

Karpovich, Angelina I. "*The Avengers*." In *The Essential Cult TV Reader*, edited by David Lavery, 36–43. University Press of Kentucky, 2010.

"*Killing Eve* Season 1 Deleted Scenes." YouTube video, 4:30, November 30, 2021. https://www.youtube.com/watch?v=U8PuZwQEDvg.

Kim, Min Sung, Soyoung Wang, and Seongcheol Kim. "Effects of Online Fan Community Interactions on Well-Being and Sense of Virtual Community." *Behavioral Sciences* 13.11 (2023): 897.

Klin, Anat, and Dafna Lemish. "Mental Disorders Stigma in the Media: Review of Studies on Production, Content, and Influences." *Journal of Health Communication: International Perspectives* 13 (2008): 4334–449.

Kotsko, Adam. *Why We Love Sociopaths: A Guide to Late Capitalist Television*. Zero, 2012.

Lane, Carly. "*Killing Eve* Showrunner Laura Neal Breaks Down That Shocking Series Finale." *Collider*, April 11, 2022. https://collider.com/killing-eve-series-finale-explained-showrunner-interview/.

Lindsay, Kathryn. "In *Killing Eve*, Women Finally Aren't the Victims." *Refinery29*, September 20, 2018. https://www.refinery29.com/en-gb/2018/09/210580/killing-eve-women-not-victims.

McNicholas Smith, Kate. *Lesbians on Television: New Queer Visibility and the Lesbian Normal*. Intellect, 2020.

Miller, Alyson, Cassandra Atherton, and Paul Hetherington. "Agents of Chaos: The Monstrous Feminine in *Killing Eve*." *Feminist Media Studies* 10 (2021): 1–17.

Mittell, Jason. *Complex TV: The Poetics of Contemporary Television Storytelling*. New York University Press, 2015.

Moore, Candace. "Piqued: Compounded Interest and the Intersubjective Scene." *Differences: A Journal of Feminist Cultural Studies* 55.1 (2024): 74–96.

Muñoz, José Esteban. *Disidentifications: Queers of Color and the Performance of Politics*. University of Minnesota Press, 1999.

Nemetz, Dave. "*Killing Eve* Boss Explains the Series Finale's Killer Twist." *TV Line*, April 10, 2022. https://www.tvline.com/news/killing-eve-recap-series-finale-villanelle-dies-ending-explained-1234818446/.

Ng, Eve. "Between Text, Paratext, and Context: Queerbaiting and the Contemporary Media Landscape." *Transformative Works and Cultures* 24 (2017). https://journal.transformativeworks.org/index.php/twc/article/view/917.

Outstanding Screenplays. "20 Screenwriting Tips from Phoebe Waller-Bridge." YouTube video, 16:16, November 6, 2021. https://www.youtube.com/watch?v=hx2fkV-WPbg.

Ramirez, Erick. 2014. "Philosophy of Mental Illness." *Internet Encyclopedia of Philosophy*. Accessed July 12, 2023. https://iep.utm.edu/mental-i/.

Paceley, Megan, Sloan Okrey-Anderson, Jessica Fish, Lauren McInroy, and Malcolm Lin. "Beyond a Shared Experience: Queer and Trans Youth Navigating COVID-19." *Qualitative Social Work* 20.1–2 (2020): 97–104.

"Phoebe Waller-Bridge Introduces Us to *Killing Eve*." *Tripwire*, September 13, 2018. https://tripwiremagazine.co.uk/headlines/phoebe-waller-bridge-introduces-us-to-killing-eve/.

"Phoebe Waller-Bridge on *Killing Eve*: 'There Were Bits of Me in Eve.'" *British GQ*, May 29, 2019. https://www.gq-magazine.co.uk/article/phoebe-waller-bridge-killing-eve.

Sandberg, Bryn. "*Killing Eve* Writer Dissects the Scene That 'Surprised' Audiences, 'Turned Action on Its Head.'" *Hollywood Reporter*, August 17, 2018. https://www.hollywoodreporter.com/news/general-news/killing-eve-writer-dissects-scene-surprised-audiences-1134964/.

Sears, Clare. "Never Tell a Psychopath They're a Psychopath: Defamiliarizing the Queer Psychopath in *Killing Eve*." *Canadian Journal of Disability Studies*, 12.3 (2023). https://cjds.uwaterloo.ca/index.php/cjds/article/view/1034/1203.

Sedgwick, Eve Kosofsky. *Epistemology of the Closet*. University of California Press, 1990.

Seed, David. "Crime and the Spy Genre." In *A Companion to Crime Fiction*, edited by Charles J. Rzepka and Lee Horsley, 233–44. Wiley-Blackwell, 2010.

Shapland, Susanna. "Defining the Elephant: A History of Psychopathy, 1891–1959." Thesis, University of London, 2019.

Shimizu, Celine Parreñas. *The Hypersexuality of Race: Performing Asian/American Women on Screen*. Duke University Press, 2017.

Snierson, Dan. "*Killing Eve* Producer Breaks Down the Fates of Villanelle and Eve in Series Finale." *Entertainment Weekly*, April 10, 2022. https://ew.com/tv/killing-eve-producer-eve-villanelle-fates-series-finale/.

Stanley, T. L. "BBC America Turn Male-Oriented Genre on Its Head with *Killing Eve* Starring Sandra Oh and Jodie Comer." *Los Angeles Times*, April 7, 2018.

https://www.latimes.com/entertainment/tv/la-et-killing-eve-20180406-story.html.

Stein, Marc. "Boutilier and the U.S. Supreme Court's Sexual Revolution." *Law and History Review* 23.3 (2005): 491–536.

Steinbeck, John. *East of Eden*. Penguin, [1952] 2002.

Still, Jennifer. 2022. "*Killing Eve* Fans Hated the Finale—But They're Taking the Final Word for Themselves." *Vanity Fair*, April 13, 2022. https://www.vanityfair.com/hollywood/2022/04/killing-eve-finale-backlash.

Stine, Alison. "*Killing Eve* Boss on That Shocking Finale." *Salon*, April 10, 2022. https://www.salon.com/2022/04/10/eve-ending-villanelle-carolyn-konstantin/.

Sulimma, Maria. "The Plane, the City, the Chase: *Killing Eve* and European Aviation Culture." *Screen* 62.1 (2021): 107–15.

Sullivan, Nikki. *A Critical Introduction to Queer Theory*. New York University Press, 2003.

Sweet, Lucy. "Undiluted, Unpatronizing, and Made by Women—*Killing Eve* Is a Revelation." *Big Issue*, October 4, 2018. https://www.bigissue.com/culture/tv/undiluted-unpatronising-and-made-by-women-killing-eve-is-a-revelation/.

Sweeting, Tegan. "The Try Guys' Eugene Lee Yang Transforms into Iconic Korean Women from TV for Halloween." *Koreaboo*, October 29, 2021. https://www.koreaboo.com/news/try-guys-eugene-lee-yang-iconic-korean-women-tv-halloween/.

Tamaki, Jillian. "Phoebe Waller-Bridge Loves Antiheroines." *New York Times*, November 21, 2019. https://www.nytimes.com/2019/11/21/books/review/by-the-book-interview-phoebe-waller-bridge.html.

Tassi, Paul. "Everyone Hates the *Killing Eve* Series Finale Ending." *Forbes*, April 11, 2022. https://www.forbes.com/sites/paultassi/2022/04/11/everyone-hates-the-killing-eve-series-finale-ending/.

Thomas. M. E. "I'm a Psychopath: Here's What Everyone Gets Wrong." *Newsweek*, May 7, 2022. https://www.newsweek.com/im-psychopath-heres-what-everyone-gets-wrong-1702967.

Turchiano, Danielle. "*Killing Eve* Creator on Crafting a 'Tricky Second Date Vibe' for Season Finale Confrontation." *Variety*, May 27, 2018. https://variety.com/2018/tv/features/killing-eve-season-finale-phoebe-waller-bridge-interview-spoilers-1202823300/.

Vaage. Margrethe Bruun. "Five Theses on the Difficulty of Ending Quality TV

Series." In *Cognition, Emotion, and Aesthetics in Contemporary Serial Television*, edited by Ted Nannicelli and Héctor J. Pérez, 160–75. Routledge, 2022.

Waller-Bridge, Phoebe. *Killing Eve, Episode 1*. Draft script. October 3, 2016. https://thetelevisionpilot.com/wp-content/uploads/2018/10/Killing_Eve_1x01_-_Pilot.pdf.

Walters, Suzanna Danuta. *All the Rage: The Story of Gay Visibility in America*. University of Chicago, 2001.

Walters, Suzanna Danuta. *The Tolerance Trap: How God, Genes, and Good Intentions Are Sabotaging Gay Equality*. New York University Press, 2014.

Warner, Kristen. "The Racial Logic of *Grey's Anatomy*: Shonda Rhimes and Her 'Post–Civil Rights, Post-Feminist' Series." *Television and New Media* 16.7 (2015): 631–47.

White, Abbey. "*Killing Eve* EP Sally Woodward Gentle on How Going with Her Gut Shaped Four Seasons and a Finale." *Hollywood Reporter*, April 10, 2022. https://www.hollywoodreporter.com/tv/tv-features/killing-eve-sally-woodward-gentle-season-4-1235127376/.

White, Rosie. *Violent Femmes: Women as Spies in Popular Culture*. Routledge, 2007.

Williams, Rebecca. *Everybody Hurts: Transitions, Endings, and Resurrections in Fan Culture*. Iowa University Press, 2018.

Yotka, Steff. "*Killing Eve* Is the Most Fashionable Show on TV." *Vogue*, April 27, 2018. https://www.vogue.com/article/killing-eve-is-the-most-fashionable-show-on-tv.

Zalben, Alex. "*Killing Eve* Series Finale." *Decider*, April 10, 2022. https://decider.com/2022/04/10/killing-eve-series-finale-laura-neal-interview/.

Zemler, Emily. "How *Killing Eve* Landed on That Tragic but 'Inevitable' Ending." *Elle*, April 10, 2022. https://www.elle.com/culture/movies-tv/a39678161/killing-eve-season-4-finale-explained-interviews/.

INDEX

Note: Page numbers appearing in italics refer to figures.